ALL THAT IT EVER MEANT

ALL
THAT
IT
EVER
MEANT

A NOVEL

Blessing Musariri

ACCORD BOOKS

NORTON YOUNG READERS
An Imprint of W. W. Norton & Company
Celebrating a Century of Independent Publishing

Copyright © 2023 by Blessing Musariri

For information about permission to reproduce selections from this book, write to Permissions, W. W. Norton & Company, Inc., 500 Fifth Avenue, New York, NY 10110

For information about special discounts for bulk purchases, please contact W. W. Norton Special Sales at specialsales@wwnorton.com or 800-233-4830

Manufacturing by Lake Book Manufacturing
Book design by Hana Anouk Nakamura
Production manager: Delaney Adams

ISBN: 978-1-324-03095-9

W. W. Norton & Company, Inc., 500 Fifth Avenue, New York, N.Y. 10110
www.wwnorton.com

W. W. Norton & Company Ltd., 15 Carlisle Street, London W1D 3BS

1 2 3 4 5 6 7 8 9 0

To my favorites, my fam away from fam, the best and beautiful Sophia, Bert, Lindi, and Yande Haitsma. Thanks for the spark that got the fire going.

ALL THAT IT
EVER MEANT

PROLOGUE

HERE is the short version. Chichi swore at Baba and he went mental.

CHAPTER ONE

AND, she's still swearing, but he's ignoring her. He's ignoring all of us. Baba hasn't spoken to us since we left England. Only to give instructions. I don't blame him. I don't feel like speaking either. Only it's hard times for Tana, but he's tired of hoping things will change and has given in.

"Dad! What is this? I mean really Dad! This is fucked up." Chichi is walking around the vehicle, throwing her long braids back as she peers into the door in the side. It looks like an army truck, if they were having a mobile sleepover. I want to feel some kind of way about everything but not right now.

I don't swear. I'm not cool enough and never angry enough. They're just not my words. I'd have to practice saying them, become comfortable with them, try them out and then make that commitment. I'm not looking for relationships of any kind right now.

The "what" Chichi is asking about is an overland expedition

truck. Baba and Babam'kuru Alois are walking around it kicking tires (as if), checking this and that and watching the gardener load up supplies.

It would be exciting and fun, if everyone weren't so angry and raw in the middle. Tana's eyes are huge in his little face and for the first time in days, he's buzzing. He's never ever been this buzzed his whole life I don't think. I'm happy for him.

Our cousins are away at boarding school, so we won't see them. We're missing them by a few days. Babam'kuru says when we get back, we'll see them. I feel like he's maybe glad they haven't come back because he's been commiserating with Baba since he picked us up from Robert Gabriel Mugabe airport. This morning Baba told Chichi, "Those shorts are too short." She muttered under her breath, flipped her braids at him as she walked away, but didn't change. I saw the look on Babam'kuru's face. It said, "No child of mine would ever!" He opened his mouth to speak but Baba put a hand on his shoulder and he kept the steam inside his own head. He's Baba's older brother. His wife, Maiguru Anesu, goes to work really early, but even if she had been here she wouldn't have said anything. She's very soft and smiley and doesn't take anything too serious. When Chichi was huffing around their house being a monster, she just carried about her business being nice and smiley about everything. Tana melted himself into her and soaked up all the good vibes. I want to be better to him, but it's not a good time.

I'm having a kind of problem that no one would believe, so I've not said a word. Also because we've all been so angry, I've felt that I

have to respect that dynamic for us right now. There's good reason. If I'm honest, though, I stopped being angry before we even got to Heathrow—a day or two before actually, because I don't really do long-range things. There's just so much going on, who has the bandwidth for things from yesterday?

It happened for the second time the night of the "BIG FIGHT," as I call it. Not during, or before, but after. Way after. In fact, even the house had finally settled itself down after all the agitation and things were quiet quiet. I thought I'd fallen asleep, but obviously not because I sat right up in my bed when I smelled it. Smoke, a dank kind of greenish heavy smoke coming from the chair at my small desk.

Now let me tell you something about me: nothing I feel actually ever comes out right then. Inside, it will be fight of the century— heart being all crazy in my rib cage and knocking itself about its walls, tongue in a kind of torture chamber where it's being pricked by a million hot needles, head being squeezed by an invisible vise while somewhere a bass drum is reverberating through my bowels, threatening to evacuate things without notice—but if you look at me, I will be still and watchful like I'm not bothered.

There is a part of me that wasn't surprised. It's a small part that only ever raises its hand much later on after all the rest has calmed down. What I saw, when my eyes adjusted to the dimness of the night light, was the same thing I saw the day the world turned upside down, and that was in broad daylight, so how and why was this strange-looking person sitting in my room, at my desk,

long into the night, smoking some ganky pipe? They hadn't looked like this that day—all dressed up in layered tassels of shimmering threads, a Viking helmet on a head of waist-length dreadlocks. I wanted to say something, but my heart got all breathless, so we looked at each other for a moment. Something in me, very far away, heard them speak—I couldn't tell you what they said, I just heard my own voice say no, and I turned away.

CHAPTER TWO

I'M going to tell you exactly how everything happened. Baba always says, Mati *mwana'ngu*, I love a good story but I don't have time for a long one, so make it short. When I was three, I used to tell people that my name was Matiponesa Mwana'ngu Mufanani. Mama and Baba used to laugh their heads off. Of course, it turns out, mwana'angu is what you say to your child to let them know they're yours and you love them but you don't want to hear a long story, or you want to sweeten them up to pass you the remote or get you a glass of water, even though you could do it yourself. "Matiponesa, *my child*, I'm in a hurry so make it quick."

Some stories can't be "made quick" because you wouldn't even want to tell them if you didn't have to, so you start with the things that are easy, like, how it was in our house. I'll start with Chichi. Chichi will tell you all about music, remixes, mixed tapes, long play, ee pees, studio time ee tee cee ee tee cee. She's going to be discovered any day now and go and be in a girl group. Tana is her

biggest fan, but to be honest I think he's just scared of her. She's a mixed bag and you've always just got to be ready for what you'll get—there's no putting your hand in to look for the one you like, on any day, you get what you get and that's that. On some days you can get more than you would really want, ever.

Normally I might tell you that Mama was arguing with Chichi about rolling up her skirt at the waist to make a mini of her school uniform, and calling Tana down for almost the tenth time—she always says, I've called you almost ten times now, COME. DOWN. NOW! The last three words are always big letters, it's like you can see them come barking out and up the stairs to bump, smack-dab into Tanatswa. You can talk to Tanatswa all you like in capital letters, it's all the same to him if you're Mama or Baba and sometimes me, he will do what you ask when he feels like it and not one second before. If you're Chichi, you can give him your lunch pack as we go in to school and tell him to hold on to it for you until lunchtime but not to look inside and he would hear every word the first time and know that it's probably more than better for him to look as soon as he can.

This kind of normal ended for us months ago. It was break time when the Head sent messages to come to his office without delay. Auntie Monica was waiting for us. It made no sense, she'd never picked us up before and certainly we'd never had to go home before time unless one of us was sick. All present were in good health so what was Auntie Monica doing in our lives, out of step?

"What's happened? Why are you here, Auntie?" Chichi doesn't chew her words, especially when things are out of kilter.

"Your father asked me to pick you up, we need to go home."

"Why? What's happened?" Chichi doesn't just do things because you tell her to, Auntie Monica knows this but that day, she wouldn't have been able to tell you if it was wet or dry outside, she was there in body and that was it. She opened her mouth, then closed it again, saying nothing. Chichi backed away from her shaking her head. "No! No! No! No!" she said, waiting for Auntie to say it was okay. But it wasn't. Me and Tana, we were statues, we had done the math. Maybe if we said nothing, if we stayed perfectly still, things would right themselves again.

At home, we went from room to room looking for her—Chichi thundering through doors and cupboards—as if she would find Mama hiding in a chest of drawers any minute, saying how it was just a prank, me and Tana in her wake, a wide-eyed, breathless tail, fear floating behind us like a superhero cape and some far-away high sound in my ears. Everything was in its place but nothing was right. There was a letter from Mama on the kitchen table—maybe it was going to explain everything. Baba walked in like a thing made of glass holding her handbag, splattered with blood. Chichi yelled at him, "Where is she? Where is Mum?" then crumpled to the floor at his feet. "Dad!" she said, "Dad!" and wailed and wailed. Next to me Tana stopped breathing. All the way from school I had felt his little body suspended in the high hope that his world had not just shifted on its axis and when that hope dissolved he closed

his eyes and let his body drop. No one needs this level of reality in their lives. No one.

When someone dies, it's the death of everything the way you knew it. The Death stains everything and there's no washing it out. I was struck dumb. Nothing was real to me anymore.

CHAPTER THREE

NO one wanted to go back to school after the funeral. It didn't seem right that everything had changed and yet nothing had changed. Even though people at school said, Sorry for your loss and all, it meant nothing to them that Mama was not in any of the places she was supposed to be, that it was a real problem for us. Baba had come back from Zimbabwe drifting. Without Mama he had to find what could take the place of the part of him that was no longer there, and he was failing. He'd never not known what came next. What he didn't realize is that whether he knows it or not, it comes anyway, especially with Chichi and Tana doing shenanigans. One day Tana was eating peanuts by throwing them in the air and catching them in his mouth, only he caught one high up in his nose and it wasn't inclined to come out no matter how hard he blew. He was frantic. Baba was so irritated that he shouted in a completely over the top way, even sending Tana to his room and muttering under his breath about stupid stunts and

recklessness. But when Tana made a bomb in the kitchen with sugar and other things, in a jar (an experiment), and exploded it against the neighbor's fence, Baba just shook his head, went to his room, and shut the door. And Chichi? Well, she went above and beyond, as if doing all the things Mama wouldn't have liked might bring her back just so she could scold her. But Baba either was not home to see it or didn't have the bandwidth when he did. I would see his breath gathering and then ebb away, falling short of the finish line. It was like Mama had been our meeting place and now that we had no place to meet up anymore, we kept to our own corners, words and all.

It's not nice to think this, but sometimes I even wonder why Mama had Tana. I mean, I love him and all and he's usually kind and sweet, but he needs too much love and I think that's why when he was little, Mama was always shouting at him. It could also be because that wasn't a good time in her life and he didn't have the good sense to stay out of her way. Me and Chichi, we knew when it was stormy weather in the house. Mama would put on a lot of makeup and look at herself in the mirror. Really look, as if she had lost something inside herself and was hoping to one day catch it unawares. She would spray a cloud of Issey Miyake, put on her high heels, and stomp around in the house muttering to herself. We would always have microwave fries, frankfurters, and beans on a day like this, because Chichi would have to cook. Baba would look after his own dinner when he got

home, but we would have escaped into our rooms long before then—quiet as dust.

When the season of storms passed, she became Mum, not Mama. "We've been in England since you were born, you should call me Mum. It's the Queen's English and we are in Rome so we must do as the Romans." This didn't make sense to me at all but we called her Mum and she stopped speaking to us in Shona altogether. Neither to us nor Baba. She even wouldn't speak it to her family back in Zimbabwe when they called. She was spending a lot of money on clothes she'd put away in the spare bedroom, until there wasn't any space and Baba said, "Mufaro, this has to stop!" She looked at him, he looked at her, and then she started to cry—just tears running down her cheeks. Baba sighed and took her in his arms. He rubbed her back and said, "I'm sorry, it's not easy, I know."

That's when the cleaning started. You wouldn't think a clean house would be a problem, but I got to thinking that she wished she could vacuum us right up with the crumbs we left on the sofa. If you were eating anything, you had to better finish it right there and then because if you blinked and looked away the plate would be in the dishwasher so fast and whatever was left would be sitting nicely in the bin already doing meet and greet with the rest of the rubbish. Those were hard days. We were almost afraid for our feet to touch the floor. Chichi said she felt she shouldn't even be there, like she was messing up by even breathing wrong. Tana would sit

as still as a post, and not even one of those that has a lamp at the end of it, that would be too bright and promising; no, he would sit like concrete inside of concrete, the very heart of a post.

But the storms were fun times compared with the absence that took over after The Death. For some time after, the house was full and funereal. It belonged to Auntie Monica, 'Nini Saru, Babam'kuru Alois, and Baba's friend Mr. Joe. Baba didn't want to be in it and when he was, he would be lost in the space behind himself or lying down on Mama's side of the bed. He heard nothing anyone said to him, nodded and said okay a lot. Even at the funeral, Babam'kuru Alois and Mr. Joe made the speeches for him. Then everyone left for Zimbabwe to continue the funeral there, except Auntie Monica, who stayed with us. It was going to be too much: dead bodies cost an arm and leg to take back to their motherlands, and even though Baba made good money Babam'kuru Alois did not feel he should get a matching set of deep holes—one of debt to go with the one of grief. Plus, he said, funerals back home are now three days at least and the kids are already past their limit. He wasn't wrong: Chichi was the quietest she'd ever been, Auntie Monica had to sweet-talk her like a toddler to eat, to bathe, to get up and get dressed. Tana was a robot that only needed someone to enter the commands. And me? I was caught up in the absence— the forever silence of my mother's voice.

CHAPTER FOUR

WHEN Baba told us we were coming to Zimbabwe, no one said anything, not even Chichi, and not only because she wasn't talking to anyone but because even Chichi knows when she's pushed too far. Baba was not putting up with any more from us. All that was left was for ash to start spewing into the air and cover us. He was molten inside. We could all feel the heat.

We took an Uber to the train. Baba packed for Tana and dealt with his luggage. Me and Chichi, we packed our own bags and pulled them along. Baba told us if our bags were overweight it would be our own problem, so we'd better listen to him when he said no more than twenty-three kilos apiece. I didn't blame him for not liking us. I blamed Chichi, so I didn't mind that we were not talking and when she asked for help to put her bag on the scale I pretended not to hear her and went downstairs for a long time. It should have been exciting that we were going to Zimbabwe

because we'd been before and we'd liked it, but this time it felt like a punishment. Also after The Death, everything was unsteady, it felt like anything bad could happen any time. I was scared that maybe Baba planned to leave us somewhere out there and return to live a peaceful life without us. I think Tana feared the same.

When Chichi hasn't driven him around the bend and back again, Baba is really nice. He's very clever and interesting and he laughs a lot. Well, he used to laugh a lot. Between Mama and Chichi, they managed to show him that if you are too happy, they know what to do about that. I think they felt that he didn't deserve to be so happy if they weren't, and if you asked me why they were so mouth in their noses about everything, I really couldn't tell you. I don't remember the last time I was really happy, but I'm not going to drag people into the pit with me anytime I feel some kind of way about it.

Baba is a boffin. He grew up in the village with his grandma, but some people visited there who saw that he was too clever to be stuck in the back of the boonies reading from candles at night. They sent him to school in Harare and then found him a scholarship to go and study medicine in England. Only he took Mama with him, because even though he was a boffin he wasn't smart enough to not give her the gift of Chichi before he left and so they got married and decided they might as well have me and Tana and create a little Zimbabwe of their own in England—country population of which was five, now four.

○   ○   ○

We drive out of Harare in the front cab of the expedition truck. We can all sit there because there are two bucket seats squashed up behind the driver and passenger seat, but Tana crawls through the connecting window into the back of the truck because it's more interesting there and he can lie down on one of the bench seats. Chichi puts her earphones on and listens to music. I sit up front with Baba—Chichi threw a greasy look toward the passenger seat and I don't even know why because I know she wasn't going to sit there. Even when Baba is angry like this and doesn't want to talk, I still like him and I don't care.

It's early morning and the city is still a bit sleepy, not too many cars on the road. I like the freshness of mornings here. I can smell the dew on grass that grows over things, even in town-town, and there's something about dust, real dust that rises when the heat dries out the morning and covers you, something dry and delicious. Baba hasn't told any of us where we're going. What I do know from deduction is that it's going to be a long drive. Even if we were all happy and talking to each other, I would probably still be quiet because I want to tell Baba about my "visitor," but I know that I can't say anything.

We exit a roundabout that takes us out of town in the direction marked Bulawayo. Baba is focused on driving. I'm impressed because it's a big vehicle and it's the first I've known of Baba doing

anything so manual. He's very genteel and most of the time doesn't even wear casual clothes. Right now he looks like someone else altogether, especially with his attention completely blocked from us. He seems a stranger. Even his face is different to me and the longer I look at him, the worse I feel. My heart starts to jump around but the smell of the ganky pipe right up my nostrils brings my attention to the thing I cannot say.

Before I go on, I need to say that a lot of things make sense to me that don't make sense to other people. Baba says I overthink things and start to recreate. What he is really saying is that he thinks I let my imagination elope with me. He could be right, but also, I could be right. Just because someone thinks one thing is right, doesn't automatically make the other thing wrong, and just because something isn't real for one person, it doesn't mean it's not real for someone else. But also, I think it's something of the opposite—I don't overthink things, I let them come and settle in my head and don't examine them too hard, then they simply find a place where they fit. Take, for example, what is happening now: Baba insisted Shona into us, I speak and understand it very well, so I know that while the person sitting behind me and Baba is not speaking English, they are not speaking Shona either, but I understand what they're saying.

"Do you know where we're going?" they ask. I wonder if I reply, would everyone else think I'm talking to myself?

"You don't have to speak, just answer me."

Oh man! I don't know how to feel about this.

"You don't know how to feel about anything. Isn't that your thing?"

What?

"Not what. Where?"

What—where?

"I thought you were smart, but this is boring," they say.

What?

"Listen, I thought this might be fun but it's boring. Later."

Huh?

Gone. Just like they had appeared, no fanfare, no shifting of time or space, no rip in the fabric of reality, nothing so interesting, just here one minute and not here the next. Not even a POOF!

I try to discover in my head what language they might have been using, but I can't decipher it. Part of the problem might be because Caroline isn't here to help me. Me and Caroline were besties. We liked to watch obscure movies, even if they weren't in English—actually maybe especially when they weren't in English. That was the thing I liked best about her. She got it. We just did whatever and the other got it. Like one of us was a clasp and the other the fastener and it didn't matter which on any day because it worked. One time we watched a Soviet animation—one of the crazy-feeling black-and-white ones where lines move around a whole lot. A mother and daughter went for a walk. They got to a gulf and the mother told the daughter to wait at the cliff. She got in a boat and rowed away. The mother didn't come back. The girl waited and waited and the day changed, the seasons changed,

the girl grew up, grew old, and the gulf dried up. That's when she finally decided to walk across it to go and look for her mother. Halfway across, in the reeds, she saw the hull of a boat. Inside it was a skeleton and it was wearing the ring her mother always had on. Then the credits rolled and I burst out laughing. Caro looked at me and laughed. "I didn't even say it yet." I knew, and that's what's so funny. She'd been about to say, "Well, that was cheerful!" It wasn't because I knew her well even, it's just because I knew. Like she'd already said it. Just like the one time we watched a comedy special in Dutch. Neither of us understood a word but there was a point at which both of us burst out laughing because we totally got it. The comedian hadn't done anything slapstick or dramatic, only speaking into the mic, but it was just ... something. So me and Caro, we knew we had a superpower. We could understand any language.

CHAPTER FIVE

OUR first stop is in Kwekwe. The town is interesting, different from English towns, colorful and not quite orderly even though buildings are in tidy rows and the streets are laid out in grids. There are lots of people walking about on the pavements and quite literally in the streets, and white vans basically doing whatever they feel like at any place they feel like doing it. One stops right in front of us without moving to the shoulder and starts to let off passengers. Baba swears under his breath. Chichi raises an eyebrow at him. He ignores her.

"Right," he says, all business, as he finds the farthermost parking off the main street with empty slots on two sides, "food and bathroom break. What do you want?"

We all ask for pizza, then me and Chichi head for the Ladies. Tana doesn't know what to do. Baba puts a hand on his shoulder and says, "I'll get our orders in and then we'll go together to the Gents, okay son?" and it's like a day dawned across Tana's face. I

don't blame him because I won't lie, even though he's talking to Tana, it's the first sign that Baba might ever talk to any of us again, and I can tell from the way her body relaxes, that Chichi feels it too. Not enough to talk to me though. We do our business in quiet. It's okay. Sometimes I prefer it when Chichi isn't talking to me. It's peaceful.

Baba knows what all of us like on our pizza. He's good like that. I like tomato and cheese, Chichi likes pepperoni and olives, and Tana likes ham and pineapple. We each get our own which is nice because I like leftover pizza, I can look forward to it for later.

Baba parks us at a backpackers' site. I see now how this trip is going to go. It's going to be a problem. I know Chichi saw the truck and how it's kitted out in the back but I think she chose not to believe how it might play out.

"So Dad? Do you mean that we are sleeping in the truck?"

Baba ignores her. He does this when he needs to conserve energy, a kind of powering down in between rounds with Chichi, maybe in the hope that she will let a sleeping dog lie. Of course, he can only try.

"Dad, I'm talking to you."

"Go ahead and talk."

"We passed a lodge back there. Why didn't we stop there and spend the night? It looked decent enough."

"It did." He's busy securing a curtain to create a division and taking down sleeping bags from the overhead rack. Tana is happily helping. I'm looking through the connecting window from the cab

of the truck. I don't know what Chichi has been doing all the time since we left Babam'kuru's house, but I've been preparing myself in my mind for this shift in our way of life. Tana hasn't been thinking about it at all, he's just been worried the whole time that something bad is going to happen. I know Tana.

"Do you mean that I'm to sleep on one of these benches?" Chichi asks.

"You can sleep wherever you like, but the most sensible place would be in the safety of this truck with everyone else and the benches are probably more comfortable than the floor."

"What about inside? They have some dormitory looking things back there."

"Sure."

"But I have to pay for it. And also I don't want to go alone."

I pull my head out of sight because it's about to get tricky. Chichi will put me on the spot in a beat.

I hear Baba sigh.

"Chiwoniso." Uh-oh! "I'm tired, I'm organizing a place for you. You have a sleeping bag and look, even a pillow." I saw the little pillows, like the ones you get on the plane. "You'll be safe. Sure, you might have to put up with a fart or two and some snoring, but you'll be safe. If the accommodations are not to your liking, and as you told me not too long ago I'm a loser and don't get anything right, then I apologize, here's another thing I've got wrong. That's me, your father. Deal with it."

I peek from the window as Chichi stomps away. I know that if

it weren't for the Big Fight she might have been more sassy but she knows she was way over the line then and that most of her sulking since we left England is because somewhere in there she feels bad. Dad is all we have left.

$$\circ \qquad \circ \qquad \circ$$

"Tell me about the Big Fight."

Ganky Pipe is back. They're sitting at the foot of my "bed," legs crossed, elbow on knee.

Let me tell you more what they look like: they are kind of old in the face and I can't tell if they are a man or a woman—it feels rude to ask because their clothing doesn't say anything of the like even though it's different from before. They have this elaborate headpiece of ropes and things that come down to around their chest, and a veil of rustic decorations and flowers. The clothes this time? Well, it's a mixture and I can't quite figure it out, but it would be on a runway somewhere and anyone could wear it and look very cool and complicated, but also like they stepped out of *National Geographic Africa*. The ganky pipe is long and almost bong-looking but not quite.

"Am I speaking a language you don't understand?"

Across from me Chichi is asleep with her earphones on. It's very long into the night. I don't even bother to try to figure out if I'm asleep or awake because even when I'm awake Ganky Pipe is there.

"My name is Meticais. You can stop with the Ganky Pipe."

"Meticais? Like the money in Mozambique?"

"Meticais as in Meticais, that's all. What do you need a whole Wikipedia page about it for?"

Geez!

"So is it Portuguese you're speaking?" I roll my eyes at myself because I feel like I would have known if it was Portuguese, but sometimes a silly question passes on through just because, and you have to accept that about the moment.

"Are *you* speaking Portuguese?" Meticais asks.

"Me? No?"

"How do you know? Is your mouth opening and you're saying words?"

"No."

"So how do you know what language you're speaking?"

"Because I know the languages I speak."

"So how do you understand me?"

Huh!

"Never mind that. I really did think you were smarter than this. Just tell me about the fight. I missed it."

"What do you want to know about it for?" I ask.

Meticais makes a very dramatic sigh, clanks the bangles around their wrist, and waves their hand across their face as if a fly has bothered them. They settle into the bottom of their dramatic huff and disappear.

I was going to tell them. I wanted to know why they were

interested, just because, but to be honest, when I think about it I'm not sure it was really going to be relevant to know. What's important is, would I tell the story or not after knowing why they wanted to hear it, and the answer is yes, so did it matter?

I wait to see if they will come back but they don't, so I guess I'll tell the story anyway. With all that's been happening, I've gotten totally sidetracked. I guess that's why Baba says to keep it short.

CHAPTER SIX

IT all started with the day Chichi handed Tana her lunch pack as we got to school. We go to Walton Academy in Basingstoke. It has a high school and a junior school, Mama didn't want complications of dropping off and picking up in different places so she told Dad we'd better all go to the same school and he could afford Walton because he made more than enough money as a doctor in private practice. Me and Chiwoniso, are in the senior school, because of being fourteen and seventeen, and Tana being ten is in the junior school. He's a ten that sometimes feels like he's still eight and a half. Some days he's all the way nine and he only ever seems to be ten when it's just me and him. On the day of Chichi's lunch pack handover, he was a nine and half, smart enough to be suspicious but so out of his depth that when he looked into the lunch bag he became eight again, so jumpy and out of his mind that Davie Cross, his sometimes bestie, told him to "calm down mate" in a whisper so loud the teacher heard.

Tana asked his teacher if she would allow him to send an email to Dad and he asked her to promise she wouldn't read it. But I mean, there he was definitely eight, because of course the teacher will look, even if she promised not to, because Tana was having a straight-out bananas panic attack. I don't even know what Chichi thought she was doing, except that she was so busy singing "Viva Forever" over and over in the bathroom before we left that she forgot to make a proper plan for bag inspection day.

From: TanaMufanani@Walton.Prep.edu
To: DrTMufanani@basmediccentre.co.uk
Baba it's about Chichi, she said she needed to keep her lunch in my bag bc there was a bag check today so I said yes but she told me not to look but obviously I did and It was a block i hav'nt checked that but i checked something else and i found hand made cigars and my friends saw me acting up and that pushed me of the edge so then i started to cry so i did deep breathing and ms Miles dosnt know but i cant email you so she i sharing this with you she promised not to look but Baba why cant we send Chichi away for at leats 1month and hopefully she will come back better
Tana yor son who loves you

I'll give you three guesses what the "cigars" actually were. Baba was well mad and Chichi was suspended from school and grounded without phone privileges. Was she even sorry? Let me just tell you how that was another story. Chichi doesn't do such

a thing as sorry. Shame for you if you are not strong. Shame for me and Tana, we are not strong. She ripped through us like hail through rhododendron leaves.

"What's the matter with you? What you got to be such a pussy for?" I'll tell you that Tana's eyes almost popped out of his head for this. She took him by the shoulders and looked him dead in the eye and breathed fire at him. "All you had to do was keep your big mouth shut and not look. Didn't I tell you not to look? Didn't. I. Tell. You? They don't check your bags so no one would ever have known."

Sometimes I leave Tana to deal with his own messes. Maybe he shouldn't have looked, he knows Chichi, and more so after The Death, it's a minefield with her. He should have refused to keep her lunch—but then again, I know Chichi, so, there's no winning.

"It made me really nervous, Chichi, you shouldn't have given it to me!"

"Why couldn't you just calm down? You had to call Dad!"

Why she even gave it to him anyway? SMH. We all know Tana can't deal with pressure.

"Why can't you ever just have my back, Tana? Why do you always snitch? I can't depend on anyone in this bloody house!"

"Why do you always have to drag him into your mess? Just leave him alone," I said—to myself, of course, no point both of us being lambasted.

"And not that it's any of your business but I was keeping it for Shaz. She's already in trouble at home."

Of course Chichi wouldn't mind getting us all in trouble so Shaz doesn't get in trouble. We're her family, not Shaz!

"Anyway, you wouldn't understand, you don't have any friends, do you? And you better believe, you're not my friend, I don't want you to speak to me. Don't even look in my direction for the rest of the week."

Chichi can be so mean and sometimes I want to give her mean right back to her, but it leaves me feeling weak to have to catch the bad vibes in the first place. She's only three years older than me and I tell myself I don't have to be afraid of her, but sometimes she's too much. I'll never catch up the years, but I'll also never be too far behind and lately it doesn't matter at all.

Tana though, he'll start taking her little treats and sidling into her room trying to get her to like him again. She's made a Stockholm survivor out of him. And it's not true what she says, me and Tana do have friends. I just don't have a best friend. If Shaz is the nature of a best friend, I'm not doing badly to be my own friend. I could have a best friend if I wanted to. Abena would be so pleased with herself if I picked her, but after Caroline, I'm all out of the need.

CHAPTER SEVEN

CHICHI was suspended from school and grounded at home. She didn't have her phone but we have a land line so without Mama, who was there to stop her from calling her friends? Baba wasn't used to doing the discipline grunt work because he was mainly at work making the money. If Mama had still been here, she would have made the punishment one hundred percent. When it came to misbehaving at school, Mama didn't play.

There was a kind of peace for two days, then Baba was called out to an emergency just after supper. He said to Chichi, "You're not to leave this house. You're in charge while I'm gone and if there's any trouble call me immediately." Of course she didn't say, "Yes Dad," like she was supposed to, she just stomped up to her room. Tana said, "Baba, maybe I could go next door to the Mckays."

"It's too late to ask them, son. You'll be fine here." Mama would have known better. Baba thinks he's at work and his children are

his staff. He lives only in one place in his head since The Death. He's forgotten who we are.

I wanted to tell Tana that everything would be okay but I know what I know, and I knew this was not a best-outcome scenario. I'm not scared of a lot but something about being indoors alone scares me. I feel like outdoors is fine, you can run, scream for help, duck and dive, you can pick up a stick or a stone, or ask a passerby for help. Inside, it's just you and whoever has come in who shouldn't be there.

"We'll be okay, Tana," I said.

I was sitting in the lounge with Tana watching a BBC safari documentary. It's funny when they take a break and do clips where they voice-over the animals. We laughed and laughed. Chichi came down and she had on full glam, high heels and all.

"Chichi, where are you going?" I asked her. "You're grounded."

"Chiii-chiii." Tana's whining meant he was going to cry. "You can't leave."

"Don't be a cry baby. You'll be fine and if you call Dad, you'll regret it. I'll be back before he gets back," she said.

"But where are you going?"

"Nonya!" she said and closed the door.

My heart was doing that thing. What were we going to do? I mean at fourteen, I shouldn't be scared but the house is a strange place without the people who should be there. I'd never been alone in it. Never been the one in charge. If you never knew it before, let me tell you that a house can grow right in front of

your eyes, and that's exactly what happened. Me and Tana were done for.

When all the "scared" has been exhausted out of you, you give in and do the next thing. Take stock. Now that we had climbed the wild peaks of fright and come down the other side, it was time to see what world we now inhabited—opening doors to empty rooms and wandering around inside them looking at things. Even our rooms felt different, like we didn't live there and we were snooping. It was kind of exciting. Suddenly sounds the house made were so much louder and more ominous. We jumped when the pipes in the wall went thud, when a door creaked as we opened it, when someone outside went "Whoo-hoo!" in a wild manner.

"This is an indoor safari," I said. "I wonder what we'll catch sight of . . ." I didn't finish that train of thought because to be honest I didn't want to catch sight of anything unexpectedly. Next to me Tana hadn't quite settled into the fact of the aloneness. He was seriously thinking about going next door and begging for sanctuary.

"Don't worry, Tana. Maybe we should just go to sleep and when we wake up it will be all over."

We didn't go to sleep; instead we stood in front of the open fridge. Baba had stocked it with a lot of treats but I laughed when I saw Tana reach for a Heineken.

"What on earth could you be thinking, Tana? Put that back."

Tana danced from foot to foot for a bit, paused, then, "Just a little bit," he muttered. "And maybe I'll sleep."

"It's not for kids. Put it back. Have some warm milk instead."

Tana made as if he had come to his senses and would go for the milk but at the last minute pulled the tab and glugged the beer. I should have stopped him but I didn't think he would drink much. I've tasted beer and it's bad. But this was a new Tana. He stopped for a breath and scrunched up his face, and I laughed at him. "See! That's why it's not for kids. Come on, let's make hot chocolate instead." New Tana pinched his nose and glugged down some more before giving up and chucking the can into the sink. His whole body shook and shivered like he was having a seizure—it was the bitter spreading through his little body. Then he yelled like a warrior and started charging about the house. How much I laughed to see him. I mean does someone get drunk instantly like that? He was just believing he was drunk and I should have been concerned, but I kind of envied him because from that point on his life was lit. He was being all kinds of rowdy upstairs banging and crashing things and I had no interest in taking this away from him. I wouldn't have minded having a rampage myself and besides it sounded like it was all contained in his room anyway. When I finally checked in on him, he was fast asleep with his legs under the bed and his head on a stuffed toy. I couldn't lift him so I left him there. I could see that he was breathing and that's all I needed to know. His room looked like it had been turned upside down and given a good shake.

I was sitting by the stairs when Baba came in. He switched off the TV and went into the kitchen. He saw the can in the sink

and shook his head. He switched on the kettle and went about the business of a cup of tea. His body was one big sigh as he sat down. He rubbed a hand across his face and when he looked up I saw that his eyes were wet. I wondered if his patient had died or something but to be honest Baba had been slowly losing air since Mama died. Work was what felt normal for him. At home, there were big gaps in the day that no one could fill because they belonged only to Mama. To him and Mama, alone—against the world, against even us. Now he had to grow himself to cover us all or find a way to make it work, but there wasn't enough of him to go around.

Sometimes when I think about the Big Fight, I see myself coming down the stairs and distracting Baba so that Chichi has some warning before walking into the house the way she did, but I was busy.

"What were you busy doing?" This time there is no ganky pipe to announce them.

"Oh, you're back."

"I figured I got the timing about right. You really go the distance with these stories of yours, don't you? Ever heard of cutting to the chase?"

"Who are you, anyway? And where are you just appearing from any old time? Are you an ancestor?"

"Ancestor! Me!"

"Yes you." As if I could be talking to someone else!

"Tell me what you were busy doing," they insist.

"Why don't you answer my questions?" I ask instead.

"Why do you ask so many questions? You already know the answers, so you're just wasting time."

There's something in me that knows they're right. I feel like I do know the answers, I'm just not sure I can believe anything I might know. If I were to try and explain it to someone, they wouldn't understand, and I'm not sure I understand it enough to make it into words, I just know I know.

"Time is ticking," they say.

"It's going to be morning soon," I reply.

"That's not what I mean." This time they smile and wow! What a smile. It makes me feel like the lights went on everywhere around us.

"Tell me about the Big Fight," they say.

"You could have seen it for yourself," I say. "Why did you come so long after?"

"I was busy," they say. "You know that." The lights dim as their smile becomes a look, a moment of silence.

"It's going to be morning soon," I say again, but my voice is a whisper because words are drying up in my throat and new ones won't come.

CHAPTER EIGHT

CHICHI gave up complaining about how bad or nonexistent the Wi-Fi is a long time ago. Tana doesn't care. He doesn't have a phone. He likes to read books about nature and science and do experiments and studies. Baba basically made a little version of himself. He's in the front with Baba, looking out of the window complaining that there are only cows and more cows in the fields along the road.

"It's like we're back in England, but without the clouds and with cows instead of sheep."

"We're in between big cities and these are farms, that's why. We haven't really got to the parks areas yet."

"Did you used to see wild animals when you lived with Ambuya? Back in the village when you were a boy I mean," Tana asks.

"Sure." Baba smiles. I can see he is thinking about that time in his life like it was so nice, maybe nicer than the life he has now,

because even though we are a delight sometimes—I feel like more often lately, we are a complete nuisance. I try to be good and so does Tana. Chichi, well, she's never seen any reason to make them not regret having her. It must be so freeing. To not care. I'm going to try it one day, because it seems like even though they are always annoyed by her antics, they still love her and give her everything she wants. In fact I think that because of that, she gets more. Also I think it's because they felt guilty. It's okay, me and Tana, we get enough.

We follow the sign for Matopos National Park and after Baba pays the entry fees we follow the signs for the camping grounds. Chichi leans forward from the backseat.

"But Dad, we could actually spend the night in town. Why do we have to camp?"

"Because we can, and it's more fun."

"Not for me!"

"I like it," Tana pipes up, he's buzzing hard. "Look, Dad, there's an animal. What is it?"

He doesn't know it, but he's saved the day because we all look.

"There, in the trees. It's dark brown or black—I can't really tell—with white patches on its face and huge horns that curve almost all the way to the back of its neck."

He's right. In the brown and green of the trees and rocks there's an animal that looks like it could toss you any time it feels like it. It's not a horse, it's not a cow or a donkey, but a wild antelope.

"Look!" Tana's excitement forgets everything except the act of looking. "There's lots of them."

He rapidly counts.

Baba tells him they are called ngwarati or mharapara in Shona. Tana repeats the names perfectly. He's got it on lock. Right now he's spelling the names out in his head and putting them in his archives.

Chichi doesn't say much but I know she's also excited to see the animals. I mean, in Basingstoke we might see a fox or a deer and what's exciting about that? As for squirrels, just forget it, you even stop seeing them after a while. Me, I love seeing the animals but what fills me with big spaces inside is the sight of the balancing rocks. Lots of different outcroppings here and there, among the trees and some so so big and so amazing. Tana wants to know who arranged the stones like that, he doesn't believe they are natural. I want to tell him giants, many many years ago, it would make for a more interesting story, but Baba gives him a little geography lesson. He isn't bored but also he's fidgeting a lot and I can tell a part of him wishes he hadn't asked.

The camping ground is nice enough, trees spaced out naturally in the spaces left for campers. It's not manicured and smart but tidy in a kind of wilderness way. There are signs for toilets and shower facilities and as we turn away from the sign for the lodge I see Chichi's face fall.

"Can I at least go to the lodge and see if they have Wi-Fi?"

"We can all go after we settle in and see what's there. We can probably get something to eat there as well," Baba replies.

"Yes!" Chichi is actually happy.

I'm beginning to understand something about this trip. Even though it feels like a punishment, maybe, just maybe, it's not.

○ ○ ○

"So what did you eat?"

We're sitting around the fire pit outside our truck. Baba has erected a kind of canopy over us and we've got a couple of folding tables and a slouchy camp chair each. We're doing two nights here—today and tomorrow, because tomorrow we are going to see the sights. Baba has got us a guide seeing as we can hardly drive our big truck all over the park and scare everything. I feel like it's going to be really fun. It's that time of year in between summer and winter—they don't really have an autumn here, on account that it's a European thing.

We walked over to the lodge as soon as we parked because it's the rules here that we don't walk around the grounds after dark, so we had a very early supper. We've got lots of snacks with us. Baba had a whole big box of supplies in cargo—I don't even know when he did that shopping, I'm just glad I didn't have to go because shopping chores do my head in. I used to love it when I was Tana's age, always the promise of a treat and seeing all the things I could have, but now it's just meh! More and more stuff and really, I can

pop in to any supermarket on my own now—well, since I turned eleven. To be honest, the corner shop is my thing. I love the one that's at the end of our street. It always smells of something almost sweetly delicious. The aisles are narrow and it's stuffed to the ceiling. It feels like a cave of wonders. Me and Caroline, we called it Aladdin's. We had a blast every time we said, "Shall we go to Aladdin's?" and the other would say, "Yes, let's we shall." Only it's just called Campbell's Corner Shop.

"Going down memory lane, are we?"

For a minute I'd forgotten about Metacias. I'm surprised they were patient enough to let me complete my trip. But, oh boy, today Metacias is doing the most. Their headgear is a kind of canvas helmet complete with camouflage from flamboyant trees—both red and yellow—and the gear is kind of swirly swoopy fabric draped dramatically and hooked with clasps and buckles and the absolute best most colorful sneakers I've ever seen.

"Where are those from?" I ask.

"Where's anything from?"

Ugh! I should know better by now, but let me tell you that this fashion is killing me. I love it.

"We had chicken and fries, and salad."

"I don't care about that anymore. Look at those two. That's nice."

They're talking about Chichi and Tana, who are playing a card game. Well, really, they're building a house made of cards. Tana will beat all of us at any card game, so we have to really not be

feeling fragile to play him. He gets quite intense. These are the days when he's way beyond even ten and could be all of thirty-five with a gambling addiction and a loan shark's goons at his back.

"You miss Caroline?"

I don't mind it when I think about Caroline because the thought appears among the stories and doesn't ask for anything, but I don't like it when Meticais asks me about her. It makes my heart do the thing I don't like.

"Where do you go all dressed up like that?" I ask them.

"For you, dear long-winded one, all for you," they say with a flourish. I laugh the heck out loud. It's an insult but it's funny. Meticais is funny. We're beginning to have a vibe. I like it.

CHAPTER NINE

"LISTEN up comrades," Baba says with a flourish. This surprises us. What in the #weregoingtoZimabawedontcallmeIllcallyouI-mtiredofalltheshenanigansnottalkingtoyou new parent is this? "What I have here is called Wildlife Bingo. There is a card for each one of us. Twenty slots. First one to spot all the animals yells out BINGO!

"Of course the race will be tight as we are together the whole trip, so it will come down to the crucial last minutes. If others see an animal and, for whatever reason, you do not spy it with your own naked eye, you may not mark an X on your card. If you do not have your marker on you at the time of the sighting then you may only mark your card should you be so fortunate as to have another sighting of said animal."

It must be the red dust that's breathed him back to life—son of the soil things, ya' know? Baba hands everyone a card and a black

felt marker that is attached to a plastic lumo green spiral with a clip at the end. No further questions, your honor, we'll take this renewed Baba and run.

"It's going to clash with everything," Chichi says.

"Your choice. Did I mention that there will be a monetary prize?"

"How much?" Tana is jumping up and down.

"I'm going to win this easy," I say. I'm more observant than everyone else. I talk less and watch more. I expect to hear something from Meticais at this point—some kind of disdain—but there's silence and no sign of them. Oh well, I think, all the better for paying attention to the game.

"How much, Dad?" Chichi asks again.

"Let's just say, it's more than one pound and less than one hundred."

We do our OMG Dad chorus that we always do when Baba thinks he's being funny.

"That's what makes it fun," he laughs. If you can roll your eyes as a collective, then that's what we do. Still it's fun and exciting to have a challenge. It's fun and exciting to have Baba back.

○   ○   ○

"You should have put balancing rocks as one of the categories," complains Tana at the end of the day. We saw more of that than

anything else, and also guinea fowl. He throws his little satchel onto the bench in the truck in disgust.

"You also didn't put duikers—lots of those and monkeys . . ."

"And lizards!" says Chichi with a shudder.

"I like those rock monitors that have all the colors around their necks. If I catch one, Dad, can I keep it?"

"Tana, don't you dare!"

This makes me laugh because I can only imagine, one, Tana scurrying after a lizard to catch it and two, Chichi having it anywhere within a hundred-mile radius. Today was a miracle in itself. Even though she did a bit of screeching Chichi was a real G, especially when we climbed up to World's View—a really huge hill of stone topped with boulders, some of which look like they could roll down any minute. Tana pushed at one because he probably thought the same as me, of course: if it hasn't rolled away in thousands of years, it's not about to do so now.

Baba told us that it's a spiritual place for the Ndebele. "So Chichi, no more screaming and complaining for now, spirits don't like that even if they are benevolent."

It's called Malindidzimu—"the hill of benevolent spirits." I've heard Mama talking to her friends about spirits and it seems to me that a lot of the time they can be quite demanding, and so many things can make them angry. So I was thinking, I will be as quiet and peaceful as possible because, who knows? Maybe Meticais knows some of them.

"Did I say that I was a spirit?"

"You didn't say that you weren't, so I'm allowed to think what I want if you won't tell me otherwise."

"Oh, just because you can't pigeonhole me then I must be whatever you decide?"

"So what should I think?"

"Think about your own stuff. Isn't this what this whole story is about?"

"It's about all of us, me, Baba, Mama, Chichi, Tana."

"You hardly talk about yourself though."

"Because I'm the one telling the story."

"You're in it."

"Yes, and that's why I don't focus on myself, it will change the story I'm telling if I keep talking about me in it."

"Will it make it more or less than true?"

"It will make it a different story."

"I'm going to need to hear that version at some point."

"Why?"

"Because you know you need to tell it. And don't ask me why because you know the answer to that."

At this point I'm wondering if there's a way I can control Meticais. Maybe if I make them mad they'll go away for a bit and let me enjoy this road trip in peace.

"Oh it's not me that's bothering your peace. You know that too. In fact, I'm actually trying to keep the entertainment factor up in this dreary tale of yours."

"Now you're just being rude and it's not funny like last time."

"You know what? Actually, I'm not in the mood for this. I don't know why I bothered to make an appearance."

"And it shows," I say, because today's outfit is nothing special, no adornments, no foliage, nothing fashion about it at all, but I'm talking to myself because Meticais was gone before I even thought the last words. It seems I did what I meant to do just by having thought it. This is interesting. I wonder if that's how Jedi mind tricks work. I may have stumbled upon the secret.

I've stumbled across something else in the last few months. You know how I told you me and Caroline could understand languages without knowing them? Well, I started to think to myself that sometimes we can't absorb what is around us and free for the knowing because we are holding on too tight to the things we think we already know. If you just practice letting go, you can start to see behind things into new spaces. Let's say you are looking at a door and you let go of knowing that it shuts you in or out; it's not a door, but something else. I mean, what is the secret between inside and outside that a door keeps? What's in that in-between space? Like the place in between sleeping and waking? It could be anything and it becomes easy for you then to know what that might be because you're no longer holding on to what you believe you already know. That's how it works. The trouble starts when you have to come back to the old things and try to let go of the new things because everyone else doesn't get it. You're left with knowing a hidden thing and that's what makes you feel like you're really a

superhero but no one knows how and they wouldn't understand anyway because you hardly do, yourself.

This is what I was busy doing the night Chichi walked back into the house to find Baba sitting at the table waiting for her. I was looking behind the things I knew.

CHAPTER TEN

SHE had no idea Baba was waiting. She must have thought we were all asleep because she walked in like she had every right to have been out. She screamed and did this funny jumping-ready-to-fight thing in the air, then stood with her hand against her chest breathing hard.

"God, Dad, you scared me half to death." At this point she hadn't yet processed what Baba sitting at the table was going to mean for her.

"Wait! Are you just coming in?" He'd been sitting with his head in his hands, thinking about sad things—I think I told you this before.

It's funny, I could see the moment it hit her and I could hear her swear in her head, like, she might as well have said it out loud it was so clear in my mind. Usually I'm not so worried about Chichi-Baba showdowns but this time there was something different in the air. That's the other thing about being able to see behind

things: anticipating the thing that's going to come, like standing on the very tippy toes of a thought as it's being born before it breaks through into the first brush of air, latching on to it with a featherlight touch and then following it out. That's the first trick to superhero powers like mine—you allow yourself to know what's coming and you don't question it.

"Wait? What? Me?" Chichi looked around as if there was the possibility Baba was talking to someone else. This made me laugh even though I knew it wasn't funny. Classic Chichi—let's start the show.

"Umm! Well, remember you'd said I could go to Jazz's party and that was today."

"Jazz's party?" The look on Baba's face said, "What is actually happening right now?" Like he'd suddenly found himself in the Twilight Zone or something.

"Jazz's party," he repeated, like it might make more sense to him this time around. He gave that snorting kind of laugh that's short and not really a laugh at all, meaning, "Really! What *is* actually happening right now?" If I had been with Caroline, we would have been having a blast. Ad-libbing Baba's sounds doesn't need superhero skills, we know them well by now.

"Chiwoniso!" He shook his head. "Did I not expressly say you were to stay home and be in charge? So you are telling me you not only disobeyed me but you left . . ." He looked upward, fully realizing only in that moment what it meant. She'd left us alone.

"What? It's not my responsibility, you should have hired a babysitter and anyway . . ."

"Anyway nothing. You are suspended from school and further, you are grounded . . ."

"But I told you about Jazz's party ages ago and you'd said I could go."

"Oh. My. God. Chiwoniso, not now, not today. Today I am not doing this disingenuity dance with you. You are wrong and you know it. What is the matter with you? Why can't I trust or depend on you?" He got up to turn up the dimmer switch on the wall.

"Why is your blouse on inside out?" I had thought he wouldn't see it but it was pretty obvious because the way it was we could see the rude side of the seams and if someone had grabbed her by the loops, they could have hung her up somewhere and called it a day.

"What?" The What game.

"What what? Don't keep saying what, like you're some kind of dimwit. What kind of party were you at that you had to take off your blouse?"

"It's not a blouse, it's a top. God, Dad, you're such a fucking loser, leave me alone."

There are days when I just don't know about Chichi. Like really have no idea who she is. She literally walked up to an injured animal and poked it in the eye. I don't know. I could hardly breathe because I was on my tippy toes in my mind. I saw it all happen a split second before it did.

Baba grabbed Chichi by both the shoulders of her inside-out top before she could walk off.

"Don't you ever!" He was breathing like air was only stopping in the back of his throat and his voice built up even as it was kind of disappearing into the look on his face—a face I had never seen before—veins popping at the temples, eyes almost lost in all the crevices the anger made of his cheeks and forehead. "Ever! Talk to me like that again." He shook her. I imagined her head snapping off at the neck and rolling right off, it was that violent. But brief, as if some part of him remembered he was supposed to cure, not cause.

"How dare you? Who do you think you are? Who do you think you are?" He let go of Chichi and a chair got it. All the way to the corner of the room and cracked against the wall.

This was the first time I had ever seen Chichi even momentarily intimidated by Baba. I feel like she takes advantage of his nice nature and believes she's stronger and more savvy than he could ever be.

"Do you know how hard this is for all of us? For me? Do you care? Do you care about anyone other than yourself?"

"Yes." She'd found her stubborn ground again. "I cared about Mama and now she's gone and you keep leaving me in charge like I'm now the mother and I'm not. You don't care about us without her here! You only care about enforcing your stupid rules just so you can feel like you're in charge of something. Well you're not in charge—shit happens and there's nothing you can do about

it." Chichi's words hurt even me, that's how deep she was cutting. Baba struggled with the fire inside him. It was burning hot.

"What do you know about anything? All of seventeen small years where everything is handed to you on a silver plate and you think you can talk to me about my feelings, disobey me and go out showing your body to God knows who and doing God knows what?" I felt the heat where I was, but Chichi was fireproof.

"You don't know anything about what I do. And anyway you can't talk, you think I can't count. Mum was pregnant at seventeen with me, so I think I know plenty and you can't tell me anything."

"I am your father, have some respect in what you say." Baba was slowly deflating. Chichi was crying, Baba was crying even though I don't think he noticed. Me, I was also crying, because even if I'd known it was going to be this way, the way it felt was much worse.

"I don't want to be your daughter, I don't want to be here. I wish you'd never had me and I wish Mum were here instead of you."

At this point, the Baba we'd always known came back and he was our dad mixed in with a bit of doctor. He was still angry but he'd found himself again. He reached out to put a hand on Chichi's shoulder but she lashed out, hitting him with her little sparkly handbag.

"Don't touch me. Leave me alone. I hate you!" She started acting crazy, hitting and hitting until the bag opened and spilled out lipstick, some money, more makeup things, phone. Baba was trying to calm her down, and I almost expected him to pull out a

syringe to sedate her, she was acting that crazy. What none of us expected was Tana flying down the stairs—I didn't even feel him pass. With a yell he jumped into the fray and started punching Baba, head down, barreling into him and flaying his fists.

"Let her go. Stop it! Stop fighting." Now Baba had to try and subdue two crazy kids. Me, I couldn't move. I didn't know what was happening. I could hardly breathe and I was holding on to the stair post so hard I heard my bones crack.

It all ended when Baba finally managed to grip one of Tana's arms and Tana stopped all movement abruptly and vomited over everyone.

"Oh my god Tana, ewwww!"

Baba fussed and doctored, Chichi was totally grossed out, and me—no one saw me. I slid up the stairs on my bottom and crawled to my room. I shut the door and pretended I'd been sleeping all along. Some things are better when they've had time to become stories.

"Hmm! Riveting."

"Oh, you came back?"

"Yes, and as you can see I dressed for the occasion." Meticais spreads their arms out and everything on them jangles and rustles. They're a conglomeration of beads and sequins and silver jangly bits. On their head is a silver hat that's strangely stylish at the same time as looking like those foil hats the people in that one movie with the crop circles put on their heads because they didn't want the aliens to read their thoughts.

"Like if a disco ball escaped from an alien abduction," I say.

Meticais laughs out really loud at this. A very big laugh that shakes their whole body and seems to come from the very first frontier of their voice. This makes me giggle, because it just carries you along whether you want to go or not. Finally, they wipe tears from their eyes; they have rings on every finger and they are really wondrous things, the kind of thing you might find in a treasure haul, they sparkle like crazy.

"Are those real jewels?"

"And if they are?"

Question for a question. This is the currency around here.

"Just asking."

"So what's the point of knowing if you're just asking? Stick to comedy, my dear, the questions are sooooo uninspired."

"They're just out of interest."

"I don't find them interesting. When you ask me an interesting question, I will answer. But until then, thanks for finally getting to the Big Fight and for the comedic fashion critique. That, I loved. Toodles."

This is the first time Meticais has actually said a goodbye. It makes me wonder suddenly if this is the last time I'll see them.

"Oh for goodness sake, I'll be back, you know that." They don't even appear for this. Just the voice.

CHAPTER ELEVEN

IT'S the longest drive in all the history of long drives but it's been eventful. We sang. Chichi was in the mood and she likes to teach us rounds—they learn them at choir to help them with timing and harmony and also just for fun. She's quite the taskmaster, correcting and correcting until we get it right. I laughed one time when Tana was nearing fed up and piped up, "Don't get spicy!" He's the one who's getting spicy, must be something about the open air out here that's making him grow into a stronger setting of himself.

If you can believe it, just as we entered Hwange National Park an elephant crossed the road right in front of us. I saw it first and I was prepared with my marker and my card. Of course, we already saw baboons. They're the welcoming party of the bush because they're right there along the roadside, doing shenanigans and showing everyone hey, look at us, we live here, this is our home and we're the ones who've come out to see you arrive, then they get up and show us their pink bottoms as they saunter off back into

the bush. They are so funny, I could watch them for hours. They are like a mockery of humans. Next time I see one I will try to look behind them and see what I see. There is a story there.

"Right!" Baba says as he stretches. "This is our stop for tonight. And you have a choice, we can stay in the lodges and you can sleep on real beds or we can keep camping." I don't mind whichever one. Chichi wrestles and finally asks to see what the rooms are like first.

"The hotel looks nice," she says.

"Up to you," he says. "Right now I'm more than ready for lunch."

We're all starving and in the last few days there's been a lot less fussing about food than there usually is with us. Usually one or more people will not want to or cannot or is not allowed to eat something, but this does not seem to apply here. Wonder of wonders, Chichi was actually happy to eat sadza the other day at lunch.

Mama used to cook sadza a lot, but Chichi felt some kind of an obligation to complain every time we had it. She'd eat it, though, and finish, and sometimes even have a second helping because in her initial protest she would have dished out too little for herself. "But I don't like it," she'd say, "it's pure starch and empty calories." Almost everything is empty calories to her. Tana likes sadza but he doesn't like it touching the stew and vegetables. He eats the sadza on its own first, and then the vegetables, and then the meat. Sometimes Mama would make him meat on its own so that he wouldn't be picking through the stew like someone trying to find islands in a puddle.

Mama missed Zimbabwe, a lot. She would come here on holiday often, by herself—not for long, "just to recharge," she'd say. "England is all very well but home is best." She stayed in England because it was our home. "It's what they know, and opportunities are better here for all of us. Their schooling."

"I know," Baba sighed, "but if you're not happy then we should really think about it."

"No," she said and that was all, that was final. I never overheard them talk about it again. I once asked Mama what made her sad about England.

"I feel closed in by the sky," she said, "like I'm constantly in my bed under a blanket. Even the sound is muted—like I'm in a dream."

I understood what she was saying. Even if she had spoken in another language I would have understood it because I felt it. I didn't feel the same as she felt, I felt how she felt, as if I was in the words she was saying. I could see behind into the feeling.

I have three lives: one, as a child of two Zimbabweans I am Zimbabwean; two, as a child of immigrants, I'm a British citizen; and three, I am the person behind these two things. I can choose. I can be British Mati and Zimbabwean Mati, because inside our house it's Zimbabwe, and right outside our door is England. I like how Mama and Baba sound, unfiltered and candid, like their pictures of "home." I like how my cousins sound, like no one is going to ask them where they're from-from.

I have two voices, but Mama felt she was losing one and couldn't find herself in the other.

I didn't mind calling her "Mum" like she wanted, even though I had to practice it. I knew she needed to fit herself into the space and forget about being a Zimbabwean mum, like, if she layered England over herself—the words, the clothes, the food, the lifestyle—then the clouds wouldn't get so deep into her bones.

○   ○   ○

We go on a sunset game drive and wow of all wows, we come across a pride of lions. Even though we are in the game vehicle and a little bit far from them I feel very exposed. I mean, the vehicle is open and last I knew lions can jump. I think our guide told us at some point that lions don't attack the safari vehicles because they are part of the landscape to them—they are used to them and don't feel threatened. If someone stands up and changes the silhouette of the vehicle that can cause the lions to be disturbed so we were all to remain seated and quiet. No problem! The hair on the back of my neck is doing the most and I'm having breathless moments.

Everyone is quiet, thank goodness. We aren't alone. There's a man from Germany and two young women who've come from Harare with a friend visiting from Singapore. Seeing a lion on TV and seeing five in real life is like watching people on a roller coaster versus being on one yourself. I mark my card quietly. Tana

is too awestruck to even bother with his. His eyes are glued to the big cats and they lie there watching us, a tail swishing here and there and the big daddy of them kind of prowling around. Chichi doesn't even realize that she is holding on to Baba.

At the viewing platform, we see more elephants, wildebeests, and a giraffe. We sit up in the thatched platform and drink the Fanta orange our guide gives us. They keep things simple here by giving you what is available. They don't complicate things with choice— well, the other choice was water so of course we all "chose" the soft drink. I guess I should say they make it easy for you to choose. We stay long enough to see zebras and impalas and we catch sight of a pack of wild dogs almost as we drive back into camp.

We all decide to stay in our truck, we're almost used to it now. No one wants to even shower. "I'll do it properly when we get to the hotel in Vic Falls. I mean," Chichi sniffs under her arms, "I don't smell, so it should be okay."

I know I'm fine, otherwise Chichi would definitely have said something. Tana is always fine; he only smells a bit sweaty and sticky when he's been running around a lot. He's been mostly calm and while it's been hot, for some reason it hasn't been too much. We'll all survive. Baba doesn't use cologne or anything like that. It's strange, he doesn't even smell of a deodorant. I've never really smelled him, he's just . . . there . . . unfragranced, like hypoallergenic wipes or something.

Caroline once fell completely under a boy's spell because he

passed us one day on the stairs and the smell of his cologne floated onto us in his wake. I have to admit even me, I was transported. How does a person smell that good? I mean, I'd smelled a lot of body sprays and perfumes at school, of course, it's de rigueur. But this? It was something you would smell if you went behind a thing to find its truth. We followed him, saw the class he went into, and started our investigations from there. We had so much fun creeping on his social media and learning all about him. This is the part I like best about romance, the forensics investigation. His name was Armando Dos Santos and his parents were diplomats from Mozambique.

"So how come he's at school here and not somewhere in London or one of those more posh schools?" This we didn't know.

"It could be any number of reasons so best not to speculate— we don't even have the first clue about that, but what we do have is a whole lot of other stuff, like his friends and more importantly which of his friends are also our friends."

"Just one, and barely even our friend." This was Caroline letting doubt get the better of her.

"That doesn't matter, we've come this far from just the scent of cologne so I have faith in us." I'm a can-do kind of person, nothing is impossible, ever. This is kind of the first rule of superhero powers. I'm also not that superhero who doesn't believe in themselves at first and they have to go through the process and train with a guru of some sort. I was born believing.

CHAPTER TWELVE

IN the morning, before we set off for Victoria Falls, we join our guide from yesterday on a bush walk. This is next level. Just walking any which way like there are no wild animals around. I mean, yesterday we saw lions. What if they're also wandering around the same place we are?

"Don't worry, you're completely safe, so long as you are with me and you remember the rules and follow what I say when I say it. Please do not stop to ask questions if I give any one of the commands I talked about earlier. A bush walk is no place for questions and idle chatter, only command and action, so listen to me very carefully at all times." This is our guide, Lovemore. A really nice man suited to his name. I feel like he will take care of us, but still, this is the bush. He stops a lot to point out things and he knows so much about the plants and small things in the grass like beetles and worms. It's a whole world apart from even the wildest garden. Mostly only Lovemore talks, so the rest of the time we hear the rustle of grass, the sounds

of creatures we can't see scurrying about, and birds crying, singing, and calling out. It's really intense. There's another guide bringing up the rear, he doesn't say much. Both he and Lovemore are armed with rifles. I'm not sure how I feel about this.

Everyone is holding on to some part of Baba, even in single file. No one wants to be a person on their own. There's too much space around us in which the possibility of anything happening is too great times one hundred, and this is exactly it: what I've been saying. Everything we see is predetermined. Our eyes show us a picture and we interpret that picture according to what we've been taught. What about what lies out of sight? Just because you can't see it, does it mean it's not there? Of course it is. We know that beyond the long grass there is something, but we can only imagine what it is according to what we already know. What if there are things there we've never seen or heard about? Do they exist before we see them and assign them a name and a meaning?

This is what seeing behind things is all about, seeing things that you never knew existed and allowing them to just be—not giving them roots, not defining them, not making them permanent. In this way, nothing is impossible. And this is why most of the time, I can't even explain things to anyone else. They just are and need to stay that way.

None of us marks our cards, we're too scared. Baba thinks it's funny.

"Shame, my poor English children. I grew up in the bush, this is normal to me."

"Be quiet, Dad!" This is Chichi. "You'll bring attention to us from the animals. Lovemore said not to make noise."

"There's no signs anywhere. Baba, what if we get lost?" Tana whispers.

"I told you you could stay behind if you were too scared."

"Shush Dad! Shhhhhhhh!"

Baba laughs, but he keeps quiet.

We see lots of small game and the beautiful extravagant birds make me think of Meticais. I wonder where they got to. It's been a while since they last appeared.

Lovemore is talking about the trees and plant life, the veld, woodland, ee tee cee. I'm keeping an eye out for a leopard because I watched a safari documentary one time where the hunter-guide was saying a leopard is very dangerous because it doesn't attack to kill; if it encounters a group, it will attack and wound everyone, whereas a lion typically just goes for its prey one time. I think it's kind of bitchy, to be honest. Why wound everyone? Just do the one and better the rest of us only suffer trauma. At least trauma you can talk it out, but if your throat is ripped out, you got a problem no one can help you with. At least Baba is a doctor but what if the leopard starts with him? My thoughts are everywhere and nowhere good all at once. I cannot say I'm a fan of the guided walk.

Tana's eyes only go back to their normal size once we are back in the truck headed to Vic Falls. All he's said since the walk is wow! Over and over again. "Wow!"

"Well! That was something, wasn't it?" Meticais.

I'm sitting up front with Baba. Tana and Chichi wanted to stay in the back and chill. The walk wore them out. I'm okay. I like sitting up front and watching the trees and grass whiz alongside. There's too much movement to really concentrate on any one thing so I just listen to the radio along with Baba. We don't talk. It's nice.

Meticais is squeezed in between us. Today must be another of those low-profile days. They are fairly unadorned—no headgear, but long and voluminous ochre-wrapped dreads. They have one long dangly earring made of brass circles that falls to their chest in metallic tassels. In the other ear dangles the feather of a fish eagle and the sharp tooth of something. Around their neck is an assortment of things strung on leather strips and metal chains.

"What was something?" I ask.

"The walk."

"I didn't see you. Were you there?"

"I don't exist only if you can see me, you know. You are not the center of things."

"Yeah but, it means I know."

"It didn't matter to me whether or not you knew I was there, I was there. You expected to see a version of me that you know, that's why you know nothing."

Did I miss this?

I turn away and look out the window until I smell the ganky pipe.

"You haven't smoked that thing in a while," I say.

"I'm trying to give up."

"Why?"

"So I can feel good about myself."

"You don't feel good about yourself?"

"Is that a real question? I mean, if you could only think sometimes before you speak you'd ask the right questions, the ones that give you the information you need from a conversation." They're not wrong. Questions are an automatic response most times and we don't even stop to think why we're asking them—a reflex that means you're always ready with a response even if it's not meaningful. I stop to think about what Meticais might really be saying.

"Okay, why do you think that this will make you feel good about yourself?"

"Isn't that what people do? Give up something they like so they can feel proud of the control they've gained back."

"People usually give up things that they like that aren't good for them in some way. Health-wise mostly. Is smoking this pipe bad for your health? What's in it, anyway?"

"And if I told you?"

"Then I'd know."

"What would you know?"

"What's in your pipe?"

"So you can think about smoking it too?"

"No. So that I have more information about you. It might come in handy some time. It might reveal something about where

you're from and link up with other information to help me tell a story about you."

Meticais laughs. "Oh, there isn't time enough in the world for that story. Which brings me to the question of when you might be done with this one."

"Soon," I say, "too soon." Once I finish telling this story everything is going to change.

CHAPTER THIRTEEN

IT'S beautiful at the Safari Lodge, high views of green treetops, sky for as far as you can see and a hint of the smoke that thunders in the distance. When we first arrived Chichi said, "Dad, we could have driven through from Harare and not slept like hobos for days."

"And yet here you are, washed, dressed, and fed. Even looking a little overfed to me."

Tana laughed.

"Daaad! That's not nice!" Chichi yelled. We all laughed. It's nice when everyone is joking and the storms have blown off. Baba two point oh was still working. We were all helping unload stuff we wanted to take with us into the hotel when Chichi did the shuffle that she does whenever she's about to do something she's been thinking about for a while. I call it the Chichi slide.

"Dad." Me and Tana, we stepped back a little.

Baba stopped tugging at the box of supplies and turned to face Chichi.

"Umm. That night back in England. I'm sorry for what I said."

It's been a long time since she's done this: hugged him, the hug she does when she's feeling self-conscious, a kind of wrestly, sudden and forceful embrace with her head down. Baba didn't let her go when she tried to pull away. He held her really tight because he knows that as annoying as she is, she needs a lot of love and it has to be insisted on her—that's the only way she accepts it.

"Daaaad! Let me go."

"I'm sorry too," he said.

Me and Tana, we sat on the steps of the truck and just watched. We're okay. Even when we've expected better from him, we've never thought Baba was the bad guy, and it's easy for us to let go of hot stuff. Chichi will suffer first-degree burns before she lets go. I think it comes with you've-turned-sixteen-years-old hormones. I'll have to remember to unsubscribe from that option when the time comes: would you like a side of angst with your hormones, click, not for me, I'll take mine without sides thank you.

The hotel clubhouse is open to the view and it's lovely and luxurious but blends into the natural space it's built in—lots of wood and thatch. You can sit anywhere and still see the wondrous valley of trees below and all around, and a sky that grows up, out and into forever. I ask Baba how come he's never brought us here before. We've been to Zim a couple of times but we never came

to the Falls, which is strange because it's iconic, a wonder of the world even. Instead, he and Mama used to take turns coming home as often as they could, like two people sharing one oxygen tank underwater.

"If you'd brought us to nice places like this, maybe we'd have wanted to come home with you more often," Chichi says.

"That's why we didn't bring you," Baba laughs. He's got jokes today. We all protest.

"Kids are expensive, and I guess sometimes we think too much about the money and other things instead of just enjoying life. It was always more important to us for you to have the best schooling. And we did take holidays."

"Brighton and Cornwall are nice, Baba, but this is something else," Tana says around a mouthful of a very big burger he's just been served. "It's like from a movie. Even the road trip. I'm going to need a whole book for my holiday report back at school."

Baba smiles but his eyes have gone far again—into the sad lands.

We don't talk much anymore as we sit and watch the sunset. The armchairs are in a line facing out to the view and Baba is reading emails on his tablet; Tana is hanging dangerously over the rail peering into the foliage below. "Warthog!" he says triumphantly and marks his card. We're not so bothered about that right now. Chichi has her headphones on and a dreamy look on her face. I'm surprised she's not frantically typing messages to all her "fans," as she likes to call her friends and classmates. She gave up after we left

Harare and barely had any internet. It wasn't a graceful giving up. It was loud and annoying, full of frustrated huffing and screaming and at one time a violent flinging of her cell phone—onto a lush lawn, at least, because that would have been another story.

"Is this the kind of story you want to tell about me? The kind that you've been telling about Chichi this whole time?" I don't even stir now when Meticais appears. They're becoming a part of my normal and I'm starting to have that feeling about them, the one where by the time they appear it's like I already knew they were coming.

"I'm telling it like it is," I say.

"You make yourself look really good, I have to say."

"I told you it's not my story I'm telling, and just because I'm not talking about myself it doesn't mean I'm saying I'm better or perfect." I mean, really!

"It means you're not telling the whole story and I have a feeling that if you do, we might see a different picture of yourself than you're painting right now. You can tell the story and still tell your part too," they insist.

"I'll tell it later, when I'm telling another part of the story. And anyway, the story won't change much. Even if the picture changes, same story." I won't be hurried, especially not today. Today feels limitless.

Meticais rolls their eyes and sighs so deeply it's a wonder they don't tumble right into it.

"What I'd like to know is how I've ended up in this story of yours," they say.

"You don't know?"

They roll their eyes again. Okay. Okay.

"What would you do with the information if you knew?" I ask.

"I'm not a stargazer, I can't predict the future."

"Which means you don't need to know because there's no point in knowing anything until it's time. It's not time yet. Relax yourself." I feel proud that I'm in charge in this conversation.

Meticais makes a loud sucking sound and I see they are kissing their teeth at me. This makes me laugh, the kind of laugh that comes right from the heart of every air molecule in my body. I love it. Meticais is vexed.

"Chichi isn't always angry and impossible," I say, "but she is always fierce. And she may be irritated by us a lot of the time but she won't let anyone mess with us. This one girl Malene helped herself to my lunch one day. Just came running and grabbed my sandwich as I was about to take a bite and pushed me down. I wouldn't have said anything to anyone but unlucky for Malene, Chichi saw it all go down. Let me tell you, if you'd never seen a tornado form behind someone, that was the day to see it. Malene was descended upon by a force she never expected. I mean, could I eat the sandwich afterward? No! It was obliterated in the melee. I'm not even sure what happened; it was so quick nobody had time to fully take it in. Everyone has their own version of it even though we were all watching. Sometimes when you can't explain how a thing happened because you couldn't process it in real time, you have to fill in the gaps."

"Is that what it is?" Meticais asks dryly.

"Yes. Anyway, Chichi shared her lunch with me and no one's ever messed with me or Tana since."

"Only Chichi."

"I guess she's allowed to. That's who she is." I'm a little surprised at how quick I am to answer, at how much I feel like it's okay.

"Would you do the same for her?"

"I don't fight but I can if I have to. I would, for Chichi or Tana. Even when we're not getting along we know that's not the reality of us, it's just situations. We find ourselves in situations and we react but that doesn't change the fact that we love each other. Sometimes we learn to be better but the rest of the time we just do what we're used to."

"And you can't change what you're used to?"

"I think you really have to want to. It's hard work, changing."

"You don't like change?" Meticais cocks their head and there's a slight smile on their face, as if they already know the answer. I take my time before I speak; it's not so simple anymore.

"I think that if you perfect the practice of looking behind things, beyond and behind, I mean, it's okay to let go of what you're used to and become something . . . easier, something free."

CHAPTER FOURTEEN

IT'S magical behind the mosquito net around the bed. Like shrouded princesses waiting for the happily ever after. There are sounds outside in the night that I have never heard before. I close my eyes and take myself into them. What is a grunt, a snuffle, a screech? All part of everything until *I* am a grunt, a snort, a scuffle, and there is no wonder or question about any of it, no fear because it's only what it is, and nothing more. No judgment nor expectation, nor surprise.

"Chichi," I whisper, "do you want to talk about Mama?" She doesn't turn around. Our two beds are pushed together under the net. I could reach out and shake her, but I don't. Even though I say it, I don't really feel like I want to do it. I don't even know why I asked her that. What would I say, anyway?

I once asked Baba why we didn't just move back to Zimbabwe if it would help Mama and he said, "There are too many reasons not to right now and only one reason to do it. We'll wait until

the reasons for and against even up a little bit more." He didn't really explain all the reasons against, but I felt like I knew—things I heard and read and eavesdropped on. I had a story about that that made sense to me but now I wish I had learned to look behind things sooner. Nothing really is ever about what we think it is. We make things about what we want them to be because it's easy, and even when it's hard, we hold on to what we think we know because we don't know that we are superheroes.

I get the fright of my life when I turn around and there, looking right at me, is Meticais. I was so lost in thought I didn't pay attention to what was happening around me.

"No, you're getting too comfortable with having me around so I snuck up on you. You're not the only one who can learn new things around here."

This time Meticais looks soft and dreamy, with a cascade of white dreads flowing all around their mahogany skin. Their gown almost looks like part of the netting around us and this close their breath smells like frangipani. I have never seen a frangipani or been close to one but I know that's what it is.

"You know, because I know," they say.

"Stop reading my thoughts, I don't like it."

"Neither do I," they say.

"You look strange," I say, "as if you have a filter around you."

"A filter?"

"Like on Instagram when you want to look better than life, today you look almost perfect."

"What do you mean almost perfect and also what do you mean, today?"

I laugh, because they are actually indignant.

"You're stunning all the time," I say, because it's the truth. "Today it just feels like you're a dream."

"I *am* dreamy, aren't I?"

I laugh.

"Tell me," they say. This is the first time they have been so calm and sounding like they care.

"Meticais," I say, "is it really you?"

"You think I have a twin? I'm the good twin?" They bat their eyes and that's when I notice that their lashes are yellow feathers.

"You didn't see it before because this is an interactive design. It's not static," and as they say this, yellow blossoms appear across the front of the gown, trailing over their body, darkening in color to become orange, then red as they fall like a train behind them. I sit up to see the full effect. Meticais props up an elbow and watches me watching the spread of beauty.

"Yes," they say with a beatific smile, "pretty damn perfect."

What I realize is that this was a deliberate scene-setting to make me relax, to make me want to talk about Mama. I feel like it's okay, like if there was ever a time I would start that part of the story, a moment like this is it. Something about the flowers and the movement, about the softness around Meticais, brings the story. They don't tell me to make it short or say anything that might make me not want to talk, they just close their eyes and lie there, waiting.

"Tell me," they murmur, as if in sleep.

"Do you know that another word for twilight is gloaming—related to an old word meaning to glow but itself meaning to grow dark?"

"Hmm," they say.

"Chichi says it's a beautiful time of day but a little bit crazy because it feels like it's a time when you have a choice somehow—half in half out, like you could slip through into night for one moment or slip into the day at an exactly equal time on either side. Like we never choose because we've learned to accept that eventually night falls. Two lights, twilight. We stay still while light moves.

"What if we found that in-between place and stayed there, like a point of axis, neither night nor day, at any moment having a choice but never making it—still glowing growing dark forever," I say.

"The horizon has no fixed point, you can't go there," they reply. Such gentleness!

"Because it's not a place, it's behind what we know—the end of the horizon."

"There is no end." Meticais opens their eyes to fix on mine.

"Exactly," I say, "there is no end."

"I know where you're going with this and it won't happen. I want to stay in a good human mood, so please let me."

I turn onto my back because these words make my heart thump thump and the tears start hanging around behind my eyes.

Like when Meticais says to tell them about Caroline. I feel hot, and salt gathers in my mouth. I turn away from them and lie on my side.

This is the story as I know it.

When Baba was brought to Harare for school by the good Samaritan organization who liked how smart he was, he met and fell in love with Mama, and even though they were always telling us that love and school don't mix, it's obvious that no one told them the same thing, or didn't tell it to them every chance they got. Mama finished her A Levels after she had Chichi and then went to England to be with Baba. He was twenty by then and his scholarship allowed him to have his family with him. Even though Mama's family were not happy, there was nothing they could do. They didn't like Baba because they thought he spoiled their daughter's chances of a good future and especially because his family was poor and a bit scattered all over the place. Some of Baba's family live in Zambia and some in South Africa and they're not so close. Mama's family were comfortable and as she was their oldest child, they had wanted her to be the shine on their years of hard work and sacrifices. They said she didn't set a good example for her sisters. Anyway, it's not a very dramatic story and Mama and Baba didn't like to talk about it much. I think that they gave us the diet version.

One day I overheard Mama telling a friend that when she first found out she was pregnant with Chichi, she thought about not having her because she wasn't so much into kids and she knew her

parents would be disappointed. She said she even got a pill to take, to close the chapter before it had begun, but then she fell asleep while she was still thinking about taking it and in the morning her mother was so all in her business that she didn't have time and by the time evening came, things had changed.

"You overhear a lot of things, don't you?" Meticais murmurs.

"Otherwise how will I know anything?"

They laugh dryly. "Little pitchers have big ears."

"All the better to hear you with, Grandma," I laugh.

"Hmph!" was all the response I got. I had thought I might get a good rise out of that one, but Meticais knows what I'm about.

"Even if you knew," they say, "what would it change? I am who I am and it's more than good enough."

"It's amazing," I say.

"Ahh, now you're just flattering me." They sit up. Their outfit is full ombre now, no longer white but stained with sun colors becoming night, and flowers all around their head, as if they have been arranged by some high-end florist. Their dreads are black again.

"You're tricky," I say.

"I am what you make me." They smile. "What changed in the evening for your mother?"

"I don't know." The trouble with eavesdropping is that you don't always get to hear everything. I had to skedaddle when I heard Baba coming up the stairs and act like I was minding my own business. I never told Chichi. Mama was her favorite and you

could never tell that Mama was not so into kids, except for that time when Tana was still small. But, it wasn't really about him, it was more that she wasn't that much into herself during that time.

I started to know Mama when I was about six. Before that, all the things I knew about anything got left in the place behind things. That's where you find yourself once in a while, and you think, wow, how did I think this building was so huge or that person was so scary, and the monsters in the cupboard were really noises the pipes made at night. Except that at that time they were really monsters and the buildings were really that huge and the person really was that scary. But you leave it all behind and build new, more solid stories about things, stories you can all believe.

Next to me Meticais sighs deeply. "Okay, it's going to be a while until we get to the heart of the matter, isn't it? I'd thought to lull you into a more excitable pace but I see it is not to be."

"Where've you got to be, anyway? What's the rush?"

"You tell me," they say, and with no sound at all, they're gone. Sighing myself, I turn over and that's the end of that.

CHAPTER FIFTEEN

WE wake up really early to go and watch the sun rise over the Falls. No one talks. We're not morning people and that's good. Only Mama was. Mama was too much in the mornings, really over the top. By five she would be up and so full of energy that it was really annoying. She would make breakfast, clean downstairs, and get things ready for everyone—lunches ee tee cee.

Right now, standing at the gorge, watching the water thunder down into a frothy mess onto and over and around rocks, in the mist of the spray, no one is saying anything. We stand and look into the oranging sky. There are palm trees in silhouette, way across the chasm, and it feels like my whole heart is tumbling tumbling tumbling, over and over and smashing onto rocks and flying into the air and up go my hands, face to the sky. This is freeing, to be water, just for now, to let go of me and have a new thought about being here.

I'm surprised Chichi is not snapping away at herself with this

background, #checkthisshitout. She's standing quietly, hands in her pockets, head bent. She can't bear the bigness of the thing in her eyes, in her heart. I link my arm through hers, she doesn't flinch or shove me away so we just stand and share the wildness inside. Tana is holding Baba's hand and his usual buzzing is low-key but his eyes are trying to grow big enough to take it all in.

At breakfast, Baba told us a story about a man who slipped on the rocks on the walk above where we are. He was taking photos too close to the edge and fell. It took them days to get to the body because it fell in such an awkward place. I think this is called a cautionary tale. It worked, because no one dared any shenanigans.

We went to a place called Lookout Café for breakfast and all I can say is, spectacular-spectacular! It's on the edge of a gorge and you can see where the river flows around an island, way below. People were bungee jumping and zip lining and stuff, but that's not for us. Not this time. This time, we're all just getting ourselves together, no one wants to shake it all up, who knows what might come to the surface. These last few months have been too much.

Tana and Baba try a taste of crocodile and me and Chichi say no thanks, maybe later. This makes me laugh. We say this when we know it's never going to happen and it's a joke we have. Tana asks Baba if we might go white water rafting. I could have told him not to bother.

"White water rafting!" Baba laughs. "No! Didn't you hear about the rafter who fell in and lost their arm to a croc? I'm not

jumping in after anyone so don't make me have to be judged by people for not jumping into a crocodile-infested river to save my own kids."

I mean, in a way he's right, because to be honest, it would be unfair to put him in a position where he has to play a real-life superhero when he's not even been feeling quite himself for the longest.

To top the day off, Baba takes us to the Victoria Falls Hotel for high tea. It's such a spread, I tell you.

"Dad! This is sooooooo nice," Chichi gushes, and out comes the phone snap snap, #thisisthelife. She stops and squints at Baba. "Are you planning to break up with us or something?" We all laugh, as Tana stops with a scone halfway to his mouth. He is horrified at the thought.

"Is that what young men do these days?"

Chichi shrugs. "Some of them."

"I know who you're talking about," pipes Tana.

Chichi gives him such cut-eye that it's a wonder he's not bleeding. She reaches over and takes his plate away. "You're obviously not hungry cuz otherwise you'd be eating, not flapping your lips." They tussle for a bit and we just watch them. I notice, though, Chichi is trying to hide a smile. Her anger is losing its edge.

In that moment I miss Caroline, like really miss her with such pain that it feels like someone has punched me in the chest. We called it the Armando Accord: the day we swore to each other that we would never chase after another boy. And I say "we" because,

even though only Caroline went on the dates, all the reconnaissance missions were a joint effort. Finding him at break time, arranging to bump into him in the mornings and after school. Joining activities he would be at until finally we managed to maneuver him into the first date. It was just a chat over a frozen yogurt, standing in the middle of the shop. I sniffed him a little as I made my way past him to the shop next door—I mean, who wouldn't. He smelled as good as he had the first time, it was sensational, that's the only word I can say. I was bewitched. I think maybe my sniffing was not as surreptitious as I thought because for a moment I forgot to move and Caroline gave me a look.

We laughed so hard afterward and also gave ourselves a big toasting with Mama's nice champagne glasses (there was fizzy apple juice in there) when he responded to "our" text. I tell you it was so exhilarating to text with him. He was funny and smart and so nice. Really, really nice even though he looked totally like a player. I won't lie when I tell you that we loved him. Yes, me too. The difference was I didn't have as much of an overwhelming desire to kiss him as Caroline did. She'd always kiss the phone when he said something cute. One time her lips video-called him and that was frighteningly hilarious—the scramble to press the End Call button before he picked up. He sent a text, HEY! and we said, Hey, sorry, fat fingers LOL! And he said, wanna do a call? I tell you we almost died. Even though it was Caroline on the call, my own heart was racing and my stomach was free-falling. We made sure Caroline pressed the End Call button before we lost it.

We squealed, jumped up and down hugging each other, and even shed a tear or two—the overexcited too much laughing kind.

Anyway, in the end, we had to respect ourselves and let Armando go because he stayed being nice to us but really he wasn't into Caroline and it eventually translated. We felt like we should have found our pride a lot sooner than we did and that's when we made the Accord because it's a real at-the-bottom feeling to think someone was being nice because they felt sorry for you and didn't know how to tell you to buzz right off.

"So you were in love?" Meticais doesn't even bother to appear today.

"In-love-adjacent," I say.

"What nonsense is that?" they scoff.

"It's what we say these days, people my age will get it. It means I was close to it."

"The lies you tell yourself!" They chuckle and somehow I know they are shaking their head.

"Where are you, anyway?" I ask.

"I could tell you, but then I'd have to kill you."

"Ha! Ha! Very funny." I'm not amused.

"Just something we say over here," they smirk.

○   ○   ○

"Right!" Baba says. "Tonight, everyone has to showcase a talent."

We were stuffed after high tea so we came to hang out in

our rooms and watch the bush fall into night from our balcony. We had to run in and close the door after a monkey got "spicy," as Tana said, and on account of being scared of rabies. I now see where they get the phrase "cheeky monkey" because it really even had the nerve to not be frightened but hissed and snarled at us when we banged on the glass to make it go away. In the end we closed the curtains and forgot about having a nature-viewing party altogether. It wasn't worth the aggravation.

Baba starts the show with ngano—that's a Shona folktale, about the rabbit and the baboon. For some reason, the rabbit calls the baboon "Uncle" and of course Tana wants to know how they can be related.

"It's a Shona thing," Baba says. "When you're older you'll understand." This means he doesn't have an answer and can't be bothered to make one up just then.

"Just listen to the story and don't question it too much, that's not what it's there for."

"But . . ."

"Hush," Baba says. "Now remember whenever I pause, you have to say 'dzefunde' so I know you're listening, okay?"

"Okay," with our collective eye roll. He gives us these instructions every time like he hasn't told us a thousand times since we were little. We even know some of the stories and the songs by heart. We love the songs, I have to say, and we sing along in response, with a lot of enthusiasm. It's fun, I've always liked story time.

Tana does a slightly disastrous magic trick that involves the spilling of a glass of water—not intentional—and some badly executed cards tricks that involve starting over several times when they don't quite work. He then decides that he's going to be Chichi's announcer and hype-man—naturally she's singing.

"Wait." Tana runs out of the room into ours and when he comes back he dims the overhead light so that only the two lamps are on. Chichi assumes the position with her back to us and Tana comes in doing his whole, "Give it up for the one, the only, the best, the brilliant, Chichiiiiiiiii." We applaud and whistle. Chichi does a wiggle, turns, and walks toward Tana, who whispers loudly, "Here's your mic."

I'm wondering where Chichi got such a fancy-looking microphone from—usually we just use a hairbrush, and that's when her eyes open wide and her face—I mean, the horror on it! How red it goes—even with brown skin and in low lighting, the red is glaring. It takes a minute or so but between Baba and Chichi I'm not sure who's more red in the face. It takes me longer to figure it out and then suddenly I know—I sort of knew when I first looked at it but it didn't really settle until Chichi's horror confirmed it. Nothing, nothing in the world can stop me from bursting into the most violent laughter. I can do nothing, tears, snot, drooling, sore stomach muscles, rolling on the ground. Baba hides his face behind his hands.

"Tana! What did I say about going through my stuff! You muppet!" Chichi cuffs him across the head, storms out, and

slams the connecting door. Tana has no idea what the problem is. "What? What did I do? I know I shouldn't have taken it without her permission but it's her microphone and I only took it for her show." Shame, poor Tana. I cannot stop laughing. I can't help him.

Baba knocks on the door, "Chi?"

"No, Dad! Just NO!" she yells. "I don't want to talk about anything."

"I mean, I should have checked before now if your mother . . ."

"DAAAAAAD! Go away! Stop!"

"Look . . ."

Something hits the door and Baba backs away.

"What?" Tana is dejected now.

"Don't worry, mwana'ngu. I'll explain it to you another time." Baba pats him on the back and, shaking his head, he sits on the bed and rubs his face. "Oh my god!" he sighs into his hands and then he laughs quietly. I slip into our room and head straight for the bathroom. I don't want Baba to feel like he has to give me the sex-and-our-bodies talk just because Chichi doesn't want it, and I know Chichi doesn't want to see anyone right now.

Of course, Shaz gave it to her. Her pocket money is totally bonkers and that's why she ends up buying things like "cigars" and "microphones" for friends with parents who monitor them more closely. When I first saw it, I only knew what it was because of those ads for personal toys that pop up when you're on the internet and your search auto-predicts "sixpack" when all you wanted to type was the word "six" and you get lots of pictures of fit

men and other random pop-ups. Anyway, Shaz is just about the worst friend ever—too confidently out and about in the world, but doesn't want to be in it alone. She's the type of friend who'll rob a bank and the first you'll know about it is when she's telling you to "Drive! Drive!" Chichi is half in, half out of the world in general. We can't go too far beyond our upbringing, it's always there.

CHAPTER SIXTEEN

I don't feel like being with everyone today. As we leave Victoria Falls, I stay in the back of the truck and make a nest for myself on one of the cushioned benches. I want the movement of the car to take me to a place that's not outside, that's not long grass flashing past the window and a road disappearing into a small section of "what lies ahead." I don't want to see the signs that say we have forever kilometers to go before we get anywhere, the single mud-colored stores with their Coca-Cola signs, the service stations that may or may not have fuel. I don't want to see goats and donkeys, clusters of huts. I just want to find a story in the hum and rocking and jolting of the truck. I can hear the muted voices of Baba, Chichi, and Tana in the front and I think of the years I've come from up to now. I've been thinking about Mama since the other night. Not all the way thinking of her but just having her hovering somewhere in my heart. I'm not old at all and yet I feel like there was a time in my life, in all our lives, when things were a completely

different story—like not-even-the-same-book kind of story to what it is now.

When we were younger—not even that long ago in real life, but a whole lifetime in the story—there were always friends and relatives from Zimbabwe living with us, some just visiting, some going to school, and others trying to find their feet, looking for jobs and leaving when they could afford their own places. We didn't ever think about what might be back in Zimbabwe; we took it for granted that Zimbabwe came to us. Sometimes we hated it, other times it was fun, it depended on who was staying at the time. Mama's sisters 'Nini Saru and 'Nini Lisbet were the most fun. They really spoiled us and it was like we had three mums all at once. Even when we had chores and Baba would say "let them do their chores," they would find a way to get us out of them.

Baba's friend Mr. Joe was hilarious, especially on Friday nights when they came back from the pub and he would be on the other side of the bottle. One time he gave us twenty pounds each, weaving about the room as he talked and talked about how women were so treacherous, especially one called Maidei, while Baba tried to get him to settle down. Mama gave us a look that said, "Don't you dare take that money"—because that's what we were always told, don't take money or food from people—but me and Chichi, we wanted the money and so we acted like we didn't see that eye. He even gave a twenty to Tana, who at eleven months had the good sense to grab on to it but not enough sense to not try and put it in his mouth. Chichi was quick to help him keep it. It didn't matter because in

the morning, Mr. Joe was not even shy to ask for his money back and we had to give it to him because Mama was there and this time we couldn't pretend not to see her talking eye because even her arms were crossed and she was looking right at us. We'd slept late making plans for that money—we should have known.

Mama's parents, Gogo and Kulu, were not a bunch of fun, so it's good they only came once. They just couldn't allow themselves to approve of anything and they wound everyone up the whole time. They complained how our Shona was really bad and said they could barely understand us. Mama tried too hard every minute of the day and got frazzled to bits, and Baba stayed at work as long as he could and then found other ways to disappear when he got home. We argued about whose turn it was to go and sit with them in front of the most boring shows on TV. Mama made us, otherwise we wouldn't have done it.

Then there was a time when no one came to stay for a long time and things got flat and quiet in our house. It's not that we didn't make noise and mess and all of that, it was a normal house, but for a long time it had been overflowing with life. It was like all those people brought a whole world with them, complete with its own music, sounds, smells, and even weather. It was warmer when the house was full, like the sun was in everyone who came from Zimbabwe and it was plenty to share with every one of us for as long as we were all together.

Then 'Nini Saru moved to America, got married, and became American in Minnesota. Mama said she couldn't visit for a long

time because her papers weren't right—whatever that meant. I thought that it was because the sun there must be different and there wasn't enough for her to bring and share. 'Nini Lisbet married a man who broke her and she wanted to be left alone afterward. She stopped talking to Mama because she said how Mama was always showing off with her great life. It wasn't true, but that's how she saw it so I guess for her it was the truth she knew.

Babam'kuru Alois also stayed with us, but he only visited for three weeks then went back to his family. He's nice enough but very bossy. Even Baba thought so because one night they had a big fight and Baba shouted at him, "Don't tell me what to do in my own house!" In the bedroom, me and Chichi cheered quietly because we were tired of being bossed about. They didn't talk to each other for a day. Then they forgot all about it and became happy brothers again and when Baba drove Babam'kuru to the airport he was sad to see him go. We knew we would miss the extra body filling up our house but we couldn't decide if that body necessarily had to be Babam'kuru.

○   ○   ○

"Well! That was funny last night." Today Meticais is wearing an oversize light blue zoot-suit jacket, with big black buttons in the front, a gleaming white shirt and cravat, and some wide-legged pants in a mauve-ish color. On their head is a hat that is cascading feathers and leather streamers.

"You were there?"

They tut. Okay. I get it.

"Tana!" They shake their head and chuckle.

"He's a nutter," I say. "So smart but so out of it at the same time."

"Everyone seems to be over it this morning."

"We're pretending it never happened."

"Of course."

"I don't want to talk," I say.

"So don't."

"Go away then."

"Not the boss of me."

Somewhere inside of me, I'm pretty sure I am but I don't feel like figuring it out just yet so I turn over and turn my back to them.

"Shall *I* tell you a story then?"

"No," I sniff, and I realize that I'm crying.

"Why are you crying?"

The only answer I can give is a shrug. I tell myself it was all that laughing at Chichi last night that's left me empty. It was too much. But really, I know it's because, later, much later, I thought I heard a wild animal on our balcony. I couldn't tell what it was so I peeped around the curtain. Baba was curled up in the corner shaking, hand over his mouth to stop the sound that was escaping anyway—a breathless whooping sort of grunting that made sweat run down his face to mix with tears and snot and saliva—a sound like dying. I can't even think about it anymore.

I know now how Mama felt on the days when her life was too

much for her. When we got home she would pretend she hadn't been lying on her bed crying but I always knew. It was like I could read it written all over her body. She liked to make things, she especially liked to cook. On those days when she was sad, she would cook really complicated things. It was nice times for our bellies but we could taste the clouds. Me, Tana, and Chichi would look at each other over our food and know we had to be especially kind to Mama. When Baba got home he would put his arms around her and really hug her, like he was sharing all the good things that he could, and she'd feel better, for a while.

"They loved each other."

"It was like they had a space that was just for the two of them inside of each other. It wasn't even for us. Just the two of them. Not like you see in the movies—lots of kissing and touching and calling each other babe. It seemed like they had rehearsed their whole being together before we got there and it became like the words to a song you never forget. They just fit."

"What made her unhappy, then? Sounds like a dream."

"I think that was the problem. I think it all felt like a dream to her. Like she got stuck on the other side of her love for Baba and couldn't be in the real time of her own life. I think because she loved him so early in her life she forgot who she had planned to be before she met him. Baba, he always knew about himself and he went for it, all the way. He's that kind of person, that seems to be planted so deep you cannot move him from inside himself. The kind of person you can't really get past to see behind."

We are quiet for some time, while I follow the movement of the car and listen to the tires rippling on the hot tar. I can tell Meticais is listening too. We seem to be syncing.

"We saw a leopard yesterday."

"A leopard? Wow, that was fortuitous. They're hard to spot."

"Yes, it was in a tree. The guide saw it first. The rhinos we saw were in a sanctuary so it didn't really count as a sighting, but Baba said we could mark it because we probably weren't going to see them in the wild. My card's almost full."

"Hmm!"

"What does that mean?" I ask.

"It means hmm! I have no words so I said hmm! Does it mean something else in another language you know?"

"It means I know what you're not saying, that's what it means." I get up in a huff and fix my face.

"I'm going up front, don't follow me."

CHAPTER SEVENTEEN

THERE'S a song stuck in my head all the way to Binga: "A Thousand Miles," by Vanessa Carlton.

"Chichi, do you remember that movie *White Chicks?*" I ask. When she doesn't answer I turn to make her take off her earphones—she's always got them in—but I see that she is dead asleep, head tilted, mouth open, and this makes me smile. We used to put food into each other's open sleep-mouth and wait to see if the person would eat it in their sleep and if not, it was fun to see the confusion when they woke up. How much we'd laugh! We never once imagined that someone could choke to death. This proved to me that we don't die because we are smart enough to avoid hazards. We don't die from stupidity simply because it isn't time.

When the anger from England and the first days of our trip wore off, Baba had shown us on the map where we were going. Road trippin'. We have two more stops until we make our way to the actual place he's taking us.

"You've never really seen my country," he said. "It's yours too, if you want it to be. I know you've hardly spent time here but no matter what happens, it will always be home. I know you are all tied to England by circumstances you didn't choose, so your mother and I always felt that you should have a choice later. That's why we tried as much as possible to make you fluent in the language we speak and the way we do things."

"I don't think Mama ever felt she belonged in England," Chichi said. "But in a way, because of having been there so long, she didn't feel like she quite belonged here either anymore."

I wanted to say that I think Mama never felt like she even belonged to herself, like she was stuck in that spot in between twilight—not able to be either fully day or fully night at any one time. But I didn't say anything. Baba sighed, "Belonging is a tricky thing, it should be enough just to be human in the middle of other humans and be kind."

"I think Gogo and Kulu didn't make Mama feel like she belonged to them anymore. I think that's what made her the most sad," Tana said, looking up from his tablet.

Baba rubbed Tana's head and said, "Don't worry about them, mwana'ngu. People can make things very complicated."

People hold on to a story that works with how they are feeling because they've become comfortable with those feelings. If they let go of that story and think a new thing about it then they have to feel a new way and sometimes people just don't want that. It's hard work and there's no one paying you to do it.

The thing I'm thinking of in the song that won't leave my head, is the part where the singer wonders, "If I could fall into the sky/ Do you think time would pass me by?" What if we all believed in the things we think are impossible; like, just allowed ourselves not to doubt? What if no one told us that things work a certain way and we put ourselves in a different pattern of thought? I mean, the sky isn't really blue, the color we see is an illusion caused by electro-magnetic radiation in the atmosphere, but we say it is and that's the story we'll always tell in pictures, in words, but what about in the reality of it? The reality of a thing is what it is when we haven't told ourselves a story about it. We're living in a mirage every day and I think this is what Mama knew. In England, she had to be a character in a story about Africans who came to live in England.

Mama did a fashion design course, then jewelry making. She started an Etsy shop—did really well with it—then left it. She'd just run out of steam and that was that. When she started something she would have an energy that was intense, like how the microwave is different from the oven, like invisible intense. One day I asked her what she'd wanted to be before she met Baba and she said she'd never really thought about it, she just liked going to school, being with her friends and doing stuff. "I wasn't smart like your dad or you kids. I got by, but I wasn't that interested. I did what I needed to do. I think there was a time I thought I would be an accountant—I found the subject really easy. Numbers made a lot of sense to me. But then . . ." She shrugged. She often did this, didn't finish her stories or her thoughts, like they didn't interest

her. I think Mama thought she wasn't interesting at all, but she was so good at the things she started. She knew how things worked together—like numbers, colors, shapes, and textures.

The time she decided she didn't want us to call her Mama anymore was strange and upsetting. She had just come back from a visit to Zimbabwe. I remember looking really closely at her because it felt like maybe she had become another person. I tried to eavesdrop on the things she told Baba about her trip, but it was like she knew I was listening and she talked in a code I couldn't figure out because I missed a lot of the words when she'd lower her voice. I think it had something to do with 'Nini Lisbet being aggressive and hurtful to Mama and 'Nini Saru saying she wouldn't take sides. I don't think Gogo and Kulu were very nice to her either. Mama said she was tired of her family and that no one ever talked honestly about anything. I think Gogo told Mama if she continued to act superior Gogo would lift up her dress and show Mama exactly where she came from. If Gogo lifted her dress in front of people, I think the whole world would end. Such a thing is unthinkable and no one would want to imagine it. I don't blame Mama for being upset about that, it was high-level aggression. I think Kulu and Gogo hated that Mama's life turned out much better than they'd told her it would, on account of her not having been a "good girl," and they couldn't forgive her for at least not proving them right, that she'd made bad choices. She'd had the nerve to have a comfortable life. I could look behind Gogo and Kulu and see that they were not happy people. I could see

that their story wasn't only about being disappointed with Mama, but about many other things—they'd had so many years to collect and store their stories behind their faces and when I looked, it was too much. They were angry about many things, they were even angry with each other, and they didn't talk about it anymore so it sat there with everything and made it dark and stuffy in their behind spaces. I stopped looking. I didn't like it there. There are some places that even superheroes shouldn't go.

CHAPTER EIGHTEEN

THE thing I like about Zimbabwe is also the thing I don't like about it sometimes: no one tells it how to be. At the bar in Binga town center, there are Christmas decorations. It's June, but no one cares and they like it. At the bar there is also no electricity—it sometimes goes for days, they say, so there is nothing cold to drink. "That's just how it is," the barkeeper says to Baba, "we don't like it but we're used to it." That's the part that I don't like: no one can tell whoever is in charge to care about making it better.

The town is very dusty and dry and there's not much in the way of buildings and that kind of thing. The sun is really serious about its position here and we all put on hats and sunscreen. There are girls walking around as if they no longer even feel the heat. They are wrapped in colorful java cloths which are tied around their necks. That's all. No sixty-pound sneakers or kicks and gelled-down edges. No makeup and they are laughing and look happy. They don't even know that this is the beginning of superpowers—

being at ease in your share of the world, in the middle of other people's expectations of Christmas and clothes, and ice. That's why in movies, superheroes don't dress like everyone else. They don't care that they are mostly wearing tights and underwear and a cape that could be a shower curtain if it had to. They don't care because they can fly.

○   ○   ○

"Tana! You especially, well . . . quite literally only you. I don't want to see you anywhere near the railing of this boat, you hear me?" Baba is using his strictest voice.

"But Dad . . ."

"Can you swim?"

"Not well."

"Can you fly?"

Tana laughs, "Daaadd!"

"Exactly. There are crocodiles for real in this water, so you stay close to me. Otherwise I will have to tie you to me." We all laugh at this because Baba really would if he had to.

We're on a houseboat called *Changamire*. I think it means a great man or something like that. It's a very beautiful boat with nice big cabins with showers ee tee cee. Our rooms are joined together by the bathroom in between them—because we're a family, so that's fine. There are other people on the boat with us from different places. A couple of businessmen from France,

a family from South Africa, and one from Ghana. It's the family from Ghana who catch Chichi's interest immediately, because they have a son around about her age I'm guessing and, well, I have to say that he is unnecessarily beautiful. It's going to be a problem. The boat is traveling along the Zambezi River all the way to the town of Kariba. We'll be on it for two nights—there's a stop in between at an island for a day's picnic and bird watching. That's plenty of time for falling in love or hooking up, depending on how Chichi is feeling. I want nothing to do with it so I'm going to stay far away from that scene.

I will never admit it out loud, but I wasn't in-love-adjacent with Armando. I was all the way in love with Armando. It still wasn't about kissing and kafuffling (as Tana calls it), it was about falling into the sky. When he smiled at me, I couldn't speak—so it was just as well I was only the cheerleader for Caroline. It was like the sun was shining too bright right into my eyes. No one should be that beautiful just because they have teeth. I could never show how I really felt, to Caroline. What I know now, that I didn't know then, is that it was the only time it would ever feel like that—the prickling in my armpits, the breathless speechlessness, the blinking against the brightness of a smile, the flip in my stomach as the tips of our fingers met when he handed me a coin to look at. Now, as I look at Kwaku, I see him smile down at Chichi and I know that my heart is no longer brand new.

Baba is sitting in the lounging area in a patch of sunlight. Now that he doesn't have to drive and be in charge of everything for two

ALL THAT IT EVER MEANT

whole days, all his tired has come to sit with him. From where he is, he can see Tana exploring along the deck—he is being careful not to go near the railing. The Ghanaian family has been very considerate in also having a son around Tana's age, Kwame, so that is going quite well. Tana has choices. The captain and the crew have assured Baba that they are keeping a sharp eye on him. I guess he has that look about him that says, "This kid is prone to situations."

Baba is also keeping an eye on Chichi and Kwaku. It's not obvious but I can feel that's where his attention is. Chichi is doing the pose that means look at me, I'm pretty and I'm cool. It comes with a flick of her hair—different from when she flicks it in irritation. She's talking a lot and all lit up. I watch for a little while, then I go and sit next to Baba. It's quiet in the lounge and the sun is casting strips of light across the sofas. One slants across my face as I lean into Baba. His arm along the back of the sofa creates a place for me to rest my head. He is warm and still and breathing quietly, carefully. There are sharp things prickling in his chest and he knows he has to be gentle because they can get so painful that it makes him cry. So he is stepping softly softly around each breath. I put my hand on his chest because I feel like it will help and he covers it with his own. I fall asleep like that, in sunlight, in my father's arms, helping him to mend his heart.

At dinner, Tana cannot be still. He has had a day to end all days. The captain let him pilot the boat.

"And then you know what?" Baba has to tell him to take it down a notch because he has lost all control of his volume.

"We can all hear you, Tana, take it easy," he says. He puts down his fork and folds his hands under his chin. "We are listening."

"The captain has a glass eye," he whispers, after looking around to make sure the captain is not around to catch him gossiping.

"He left me and Kwame in the control room but he took his glass eye out, put it in a glass, and said, "I'll be right back," then he pointed at the eye and said, "I'll be watching you." Tana can barely tell the story now, he is laughing so much. Holding his stomach, he gasps, "Baba, can you imagine! He said he was watching us." He laughs and laughs. "Kwame didn't like it, he took off his hat and covered it. 'Let him watch that,' he said."

Kwame leans into the story from farther down the table. "There could have been a camera in that eye, you know. They put cameras in everything these days."

Tana's eyes grow and his mouth makes an O. "I never thought of that." He grabs his plate and scoots down to squeeze himself between Kwame and Kwaku. Kwaku gets up to give Tana his seat and comes to sit next to Chichi. He greets Baba politely and Baba only nods before turning to say something to Kwaku and Kwame's parents.

I said I would stay away from the scene, but I cannot. Kwaku is easy to see behind. I allow myself to let go of what I think I know about him, all the thoughts about his smile, his smooth skin, his voice, and I let the things that he's about find me in the space I create for them.

Kwaku reads a lot and that's what helps him in school. He studies hard because he wants his parents to be proud of him. He's an athlete and loves the things he can push his body to do, he pushes himself further and further every time he trains. He wants his body to be a machine, like the suits Iron Man wears, so that all he has to do is fit himself with a cape and a costume. He will be successful, but he will never fly because he's written his story from beginning to end and he's left no room for the reality of who he is.

Chichi could float away any minute because she has not thought beyond the next word that is leaving her mind. She could be anything, do anything, from one minute to the next, and that is why Baba is on red alert. The mood has been good for a while now. We're slipping into the new us and it's comfortable, but no one should think of getting too cozy. We have to remember that we are the kind of people for whom a sunny day can become stormy from one minute to the next.

It's not that I'm psychic or a mind reader or anything tricky like that, I just don't defeat my thoughts with logic. If they come into my head I accept them. That's the simple instruction on how to look behind things. It's not easy to do, it takes practice. Me and Caroline, we took the time to practice this and we got really good at it.

For some reason, at this very point in my thoughts I'm expecting Meticais but they don't make an appearance. Maybe because last time I said, "Don't follow me." Maybe because they're

busy creating an outfit and it's taking longer than usual. This thought makes me laugh. I can't imagine Meticais actually sitting down to create those out of this-world outfits. "Who, me?" they'd say. "Really, what could you be thinking? Tell me another story, and make it a good one."

CHAPTER NINETEEN

IT'S strange to sleep on the water and be so close to it. I think it's different on a ship because it's so high out of the water. Not so on a houseboat. You literally walk off a gangplank onto land and if they leave it down, even a crocodile can climb right onto the deck. I'm imagining that now, as I lie in the dark. It's late. There's a plopping, bubble-popping sound coming from the water outside. Then a snort of some sort. Hippos having a laugh, I think, then I laugh to myself at that; or a crocodile choking on a feather. It's fun to imagine these things. Hippos always seem to be in a gang, just hanging out in the water, so it makes sense that at some point they'd have a laugh about something, and crocs always seem to have a bird nearby—well, in pictures, in any case. A pod of hippos, I think, as my mind starts to slip into a haze. I'm sleepier than usual this evening. It was the sun and letting Baba's tired heart be a part of mine. Even at dinner, I just listened.

On the very edge of sleep I feel Chichi leave her bed. I open my eyes as much as they will let me and see her silhouette slip out the door. Next time I open them I see Meticais, sitting in the chair next to my bed, holding their pipe and watching me. It all feels so strange today, Meticais has a glittery red mask that leaves only their eyes, nose, and mouth free. Their dreads look like they are wrapped with silver tinsel and I hear a slight rustle as their head moves. We look at each other in silence for the brief minute my eyes are open. Just look, and then my eyes close again. I don't even form the thought of asking where they've been, I'm drifting all the way into the confusion of dreams. Somewhere way back in the distance I think that I hear the door to Baba's cabin open and close. He knows, I think. He was on red alert.

When I wake up again it feels like I've slept for years and gone to so many different places in my dreams, but in reality it's only been the time it took for Chichi to leave and for Baba to figure out that she had left, follow her, find her, and bring her back to our rooms. I know all this the minute I wake up, like even though I was asleep I was aware of everything—like when a computer sleeps but the apps are still updating in the background. I don't question the things I know anymore, so you just have to accept this about me.

Chichi stomps into the room and throws something on the bed. I feel Baba's shadow in the doorway. They keep their voices low. Except these days, it's like I don't sleep, I do a worldwide tour of dreamscapes and wake up any old time, like now.

Chichi throws herself onto the bed with a huff and I feel Baba take the seat on the other side of the bed.

"Oh my days! That was so embarrassing, Dad. Did you really have to do that?"

I know that Baba has leaned forward and is rubbing his face in his hands before he speaks, I even hear him breathe out deeply before he does. He's a creature of habit, this father of ours. It's easy to learn him so well that you never have to be surprised. I'm surprised Chichi has forgotten this about him. To be honest, though, Chichi isn't thinking too much about anything these days. When I look behind her story I keep seeing a small speck in wide open water, bobbing about, wondering if there's a shark beneath her and telling herself all the things she would do to fight it and survive. She's not even thinking if there is land on the horizon or if a ship will pass by.

"Chiwoniso, I'm your father, I will always do what is my duty toward you. You don't know that boy. You shouldn't have snuck out to meet him and you shouldn't have been drinking. Anything could have happened to you."

"Well, nothing happened," Chichi mumbles.

"Chi . . ."

"Nothing happened, Dad! Okay. We only kissed a little bit."

Baba sighs.

"Are you sexually active?"

"I don't want to talk to you about this."

"That's too bad, because you've made it necessary."

"You gave me that whole doctor's talk last year, Dad! I know

about pregnancy and diseases and all that. You don't have to tell me about that."

I was there for that talk. It was disturbing. I wouldn't want to have it again. Maybe a different kind of talk.

"Okay, it's good that you remember that. But as your parent I'm going to need to know, because I have to be able to trust you when you're out of the house."

Chichi's voice almost disappears when she mumbles the words, "Only once."

Then there is silence. I know Baba is measuring and weighing in his head. His face needs another rub before he speaks because it helps him relax his brain after too much rapid calculation.

"With whom?"

"A boy from school."

"That night you snuck out?"

"No, at a party, one you let me go to."

"Okay. Did you use protection?"

"Yes, Dad!"

"Is this boy your boyfriend?"

"No." Chichi's voice is disappearing. I can hardly hear her answers. She knows what Baba really means by that question. Baba doesn't say anything. Chichi sniffles. Her head is down.

"He didn't even speak to me again after." She sniffs again. And again. She's crying.

"And this boy Kwaku. What were your intentions in meeting him?"

She shrugs, and Baba hands her a tissue from the box on the bedside thingy.

"I don't know. I just thought it might be fun. I don't know. Just to do something."

This is the quietest conversation ever in the world of Chichi and Baba. Something that hasn't happened in the history of Chichi and Baba chats. When they are happy and being silly, they laugh and joke really loudly and fool around like pals (not in a long time though), and the rest of the time they are arguing and yelling or loudly ignoring each other—and we all suffer. Chichi sniffs and blows her nose while Baba thinks. Then finally, he says, "I should probably have told you this before. Even though we hadn't planned on having a baby, we wanted you. We were excited."

"You weren't married, though, and she was still so young. You were nineteen, Dad, you should have known better."

"We wanted to get married and we knew your mother's family would never agree. I had nothing, my family were nobodies, but I knew where I was going and I was sure of what I could accomplish. We wanted to be together. When I met your mother, that was it for me. I was never a person who couldn't make their mind up. I always knew what I wanted when I saw it, and what wasn't for me, wasn't for me. It was never complicated, and your mother knew that. She was sure of me and I was sure of her."

"But she was so unhappy, though. Maybe you just thought you knew. People don't fall in love like that, that only happens in the movies."

"Your mum was . . . complicated. It's not anything you would understand, nobody can really, but I knew I loved her . . . Look, the reason I am telling you this, is so you know you are not a mistake we failed to fix, you are not responsible for how anything turned out. You can be angry about other things, but not about that. We wanted you, we were happy when you were born, and we have loved you through every moment of your life, including this one."

Somewhere in a corner of my mind I think of the conversation I overheard, but I will never say anything to Chichi. Just because someone wasn't sure about something one time, doesn't mean anything. I don't blame Mama for having had doubts. Watching Chichi with Kwaku that afternoon I had thought, in a year, Chichi will be Mama, pregnant, not having finished school, and worried about what her parents will say. In the year after that she will find herself with a baby and a husband in a new country, and in the next sixteen years she will try to find herself behind two more children and all they bring, without a chance to be herself for herself, without the chance to look behind her parents, behind her husband, behind her children to learn her true superpower. Half her life in one place, in one hemisphere and the other half on the other side of everything, she would always be too far from the center on either side.

"You used me to get what you wanted," Chichi says finally. She had to take some time to decide if she was going to accept Baba's words.

"No, you were the cherry on the cake." Baba is smiling because Chichi is coming back to herself. This was a steep walk for them, and it happened because when Baba sat on the sofa in the sun and listened to the heaviness of his heart, he looked at Chichi flicking her hair at Kwaku and knew that if she went around a corner, this time he was going to lose sight of her.

CHAPTER TWENTY

THE next day is special because it's Tana's birthday. He is hip-hopping about all over the place and cannot be still for a second. He is so happy and this makes us all happy too. Baba and Chichi are in a strangely quiet space, like their conversation in the night has left them not quite sure how to be around each other. They give all the attention to Tana. They reached an agreement, that Chichi was not to have any more sexual activity with boys unless they were in a serious relationship and had been dating for at least five months. Baba had said a year but I know he was playing street salesman so he could have bargaining room. And also he said at three months he would like to meet the boy but not before, just in case she changed her mind—he doesn't want a parade of young men coming to meet him because otherwise this would make him think that he didn't raise Chichi right.

I feel like I slept in a deep and soothing pool of some kind of balm. I didn't hear Baba leave the room or Chichi settle into bed. I don't

even know if I heard the end of the conversation because last night, sleep was really being the boss of me. The dreams were too much. I feel them on the very edge of my mind but I can't remember them properly. Those are the dreams that make a comeback unexpectedly and then I can't figure out if it's a new thought or part of a dream. This birthday of Tana's has started to feel like that kind of dream you wake up from and think, "Oh my days! That felt like a movie."

We are on the small beach of the island, keeping a beady eye for crocodiles and other wildlife, after a really nice lunch, with cake in honor of Tana's birthday. Somehow, Baba managed to arrange that with the captain before we came; I'm beginning to realize this trip wasn't just an impromptu decision for him because of some big fight. It's crazy how one thing can take you in a direction of thought that's not even the truth. Now that the effects of the Big Fight have worn off, I can see everything more clearly.

Anyway, we are told to get back on the boat without delay because there are lions in the area. Imagine! Actual lions roaming about in the place where we were hanging about having drinks and things. But as if that weren't enough of the surreal, we watch as the lions take down a kudu, three of them. It's brutal and strangely beautiful to see with our own eyes something we've only ever seen on television. My heart is hammering. Tana is outside of himself completely—he asks Baba to put him on his shoulders so he can record on the phone. No one moves on that top deck, I'm not even sure if we are all still breathing for the time it takes to bring the animal down. The sounds make the hairs all over my body

rise like I'm also in danger. Chichi digs her nails into Baba's arm, whispering, "Dad! Dad! Oh my gosh!" the whole time.

That's the end of getting off the boat for us, because after that comes hyenas. We don't see them, just hear them in the bushes. One of the guides on the boat tells us that lions and hyenas are enemies for life, like street gangs, because they're always coming onto each other's turf. Tana wants to see a fight between them, "Baba, that would be really brilliant!" he says. He looks like a kid who's eaten a whole bunch of spiked sugar or something, like he could take off flying any minute: overly bright eyes, looking like he's running a fever. He's been given his whole life today.

"Look, Baba!" He's playing his video. We all lean in. It's surprisingly good quality, I would have thought he'd be all shaky and the picture blurry, but it turns out the boy has skills. Go Tana!

He actually looks a year older. Beaming, he presses replay on the video. There's no denying him his eleven years today. It's like on this trip he's growing in real time.

It's been gorgeous weather since we've been here and today is no exception. The sky is open and endless, the sun is warm without being too hot and sometimes there's a nice breeze blowing. Chichi and Kwaku are sitting across from each other at one of the outdoor tables on the deck and Baba is having a drink with the other men. What's funny is that everyone joined in for Tana's birthday so it was like an actual party, only with strangers who are friends because of being in such close quarters together. It was nice, really easy and light. But for me, it wasn't his best birthday.

When Tana turned eight Mama cooked the biggest, best feast of a birthday. We had all his friends and some of ours as well. All day the party spilled from the house into the yard. I don't know how Mama did it—the decorations, the food, I mean she cooked and planned for a whole two weeks. It was so much fun because for that day there didn't seem to be any rules. Us older children ran riot, playing music and dancing, Chichi and her friends put makeup on and spritzed and primped all day, and when it was all over we were exhausted and the house was a mess. Tana was knocked out. Baba had to go to an emergency. We started to clean up but Mama said leave it, we'll do it later, let's have a break. She made our favorite mixed sugar and salted popcorn—a big bowl. She shut the doors to outside, pulled a throw from the sofa, and said sit. Me and Chichi, we sat on either side of her, ate popcorn, and watched an eighties movie called *The Last Dragon*, and then *Coming to America*. Mama loved Eddie Murphy. We weren't really paying all our attention to the movie, we were talking a lot about what had happened during the day, what was happening in the movie, and laughing at Mama when she told us how Baba had "courted" her. We laughed mainly at the word "courted." She said, "Of course he did. He was so forward but also very charming and sweet and patient." This made us laugh even more. Baba! "What would you know, you guys just say, 'Hey what's up, what's up!'" I don't know why but all this was so hilarious. Me and Chichi laughed so much we rolled off the sofa and into each other's arms on the floor. Then for some reason we started throwing popcorn at each other. It was a mess and we left it like

that. By the time we woke up the next morning, Mama had cleaned everything and we went back to our routine of good day, bad day.

"You see how you are?"

I almost cry out in happiness. Meticais!

"You're back!"

"I never went anywhere."

"You've been quite absent."

"I've been unobtrusive, there's a difference."

"Why?"

"Is a letter that comes after X and before Z."

It takes me a brief second.

"Ahh, come on, don't be like that. And anyway, that's a really old one." I laugh because it's just a really silly joke.

They shrug. "All this time I've been asking for you to tell me another part of the story and you start it when I'm not there. I see what you're doing though, you wanted me to come back."

They smirk and wink. "I got your number, kid."

Today they are dressed in a long orange smock with a beaded leather waistcoat. Their dreads are caked in red ochre again and there is a pair of ginormous rhinestone studded sunglasses on their face. Dangling from one ear is a blingy chandelier earring and on the other side, a cascade of beaten silver rings joined together. The bejeweled rings are back on every finger and the ganky pipe is in one hand.

"You're smoking again."

"What sharp eyes you have."

I give them stank eye, and they laugh. "I missed it—my pipe.

Started asking why I should put myself through missing something if I didn't absolutely have to."

"I guess there's enough things to miss because you have no choice, no point in making things harder for yourself if there's no real need."

"You're beginning to miss her now, aren't you? You haven't wanted to talk about yourself in the story because you know you're angry too, and you feel like it's too much if you and Chichi are both acting out. You don't have to be the sensible one, you know. I thought you were the one who didn't hold on to things."

"That's different," I say. I'm wondering why I even thought I missed Meticais.

"I don't have to be here, you know."

"So go."

"I could, but I already packed for the trip and I didn't bring all these looks out here for nothing."

"Where do you come from, anyway?"

"You tell me."

"Ugh!" I honestly can't be bothered with them sometimes.

"Oh, it's okay for you to be saucy with me, but with everyone else you play the good girl."

"I do not."

"Oh yeah! Chichi did this, Chichi did that, Tana is like this, Tana is like that. Me, I'm perfect."

"Go away, honestly, just go away and this time don't come back."

CHAPTER TWENTY-ONE

I never said I was perfect. In fact I can be a bit of hard work, just in a different way than Chichi. For instance, even though I don't follow the rules of the way things are, I really don't like it when people break the rules we've agreed on together. Fair is fair.

I go to a special after-school program twice a week, because the teachers say I think differently from a lot of people. Some things make perfect sense to me and others don't. I have to practice letting them make sense and we do mental exercises there that help to make my thoughts work with those of everyone else. They also give me puzzles and things that test to see how much I know that they don't know. On these days, Mama usually picks me up. After the program—in fact that's what it's called, The Program—we sometimes go and have coffee and cake.

This day, we went to a café she liked where she was friends with the chef. It was warmly lit in there and it made me feel like I was somewhere really special, but in a way that wasn't

complicated. You could be yourself there, any way you wanted to be, and feel right at home. Mama looked through her menu for a long time then ordered lemonade for both of us and Caesar salad with chicken and bacon chips—sometimes it's more than coffee and cake—then she looked at me for a long time and I looked back at her.

"What people don't know about you is that you like to tell stories but you're not a great talker. It's a strange thing, you would think that one can't be without the other, but somehow you seem to do it."

"It's because the stories are real. If I just talk then it's only bits and pieces, like I'm leaking stuff. I need to put it all together first."

"I hope," she said, and stopped to think first about how to say what she hoped. "I hope that you will find someone who understands how special you are. Complicated, interesting, and so . . ."

"So what?" She stroked my face and hummed a little hmm.

"Your father had that same look in his eyes, like he knew things. It made me want to know him."

"And did you?"

"That's the thing," she said, "one of the things he knew turned out to be me. That's what drew me to him, he knew me."

I knew then that what she was saying was, sometimes what we see in others is what we're looking for in ourselves. She wanted him to help her to know herself the way he knew her, but that's the thing: if she couldn't find it out for herself, no matter what he

told her, he might as well have been speaking a language she would never understand.

Another time, completely out of the blue, she said, "Never sleep with a boy if you don't know that he will be nice to you the next time you see him." I wasn't sure it was the time to tell me about sleeping with boys, but Mama was like that—she could be really random. I couldn't imagine such a thing. When we fell in love with Armando, I never once thought of anything other than just feeling in love. I liked how it felt and that was the whole thing for me. Maybe because it was easy to leave the other feelings to Caroline. It felt like he was hers anyway, so I didn't have any responsibility for that part. She didn't sleep with him—it was tough but we realized he never liked her like that. He only kissed her, on both cheeks all the time, as if he was saying hello or goodbye to his aunt or grandmother. We didn't care though. It was contact and we felt like we were flying those days. Sometimes I'm not sure of my sanity when it comes to the story of Armando. It seems crazy and the feelings were wild, but I think what it really was, was safe. When it's not your story, you can be in it however you want and it won't just about kill you when it goes wrong and it's easy to talk about.

I don't even break my stride now. I know it like I know my next thought, Meticais is here.

"She should have told Chichi that about boys."

"How do you know she didn't?" they say.

I shrug.

"She would have listened, I think. It was the way Mama said it to me that made me believe her. Chichi thinks she's really cool but we can't help ourselves, there are some things Mama and Baba say that don't leave us even when we think we're being rebels."

"Is that so?"

"You know it's so. Isn't that why they say, the apple doesn't fall far from the tree?"

"I don't know, you tell me," they say.

"I'm telling you," I say.

"Okay then."

"How come you're back, anyway? We had a tiff and I told you to go away."

"But I didn't, did I? See? Here I still am."

I can't help it, I laugh. I really don't understand this person but for some reason it's comforting to know that there is someone around me who is this unfettered. Things that exist outside boundaries give me comfort, not things that are within boundaries trying to break out. It's too much conflict, it makes me anxious. Sometimes I feel like two people—one who has to walk within the lines and another who doesn't know about lines. The two don't really work unless they stay back to back and do what works on their side.

"I've never been more or less than what I am," Meticais says, "I have always just been."

"Lucky you," I say. I don't even bother to ask again where they come from and what their life might be like there. I am starting

to understand that the reason they are hanging around me is not about them. They are waiting for something and it's got to do with the story I've been telling. I'm having a faraway feeling that I know what it is and it's making my heart do the thing I don't like.

"I have to go and join the game of cards," I say, and I get up from the sofa to go out onto the deck.

"Is that right?"

"Yes," I say, "that's exactly right."

The boat trip doesn't pace itself. After Tana's birthday and Chichi's shenanigans of the night before, not much else happens. We play cards, we eat, the adults have drinks and talk about things in the world, we hang out, read, play games on our phones, watch the water. Kwaku is actually nice and funny. There's no more funny business with him and Chichi. It's like she's stopped throwing herself against walls inside herself, she's really calm and they seem to be becoming real friends. Kwame and Tana have the run of the boat, having the time of their lives. The night is uneventful, everyone stays in their beds, and we arrive at Kariba in the morning. Lo and behold, our truck is there to meet us. We have such a laugh. For some reason we'd thought that the last we'd see of it was when we left it at Binga, but Dad hired someone to drive it to Kariba for us while we were on the houseboat.

We drive to the dam wall and walk for a bit, looking at how high up from the water we are. It's nothing special, but it feels strange after being two days on water, to be back on land, like everything is tilting. I like how it feels—like nothing is sure or

determined and at any moment the ground could tip you right up and off. When things around me aren't fully decided of themselves like this, it makes me happy because it means if you don't like how something is, it can possibly change.

Meticais is on the dam with us, but they act like they don't know me. They walk down the length of the bridge and back with a bright yellow cloak floating behind them, as if they're on a runway. Their dreads are coiled up and entwined in a huge crown of sunflowers, eyes behind very big dark sunglasses. They have a Nyaminyami walking stick with a blingy gold head and this, they hold aloft like a scepter. I try to hail them but they sweep past me in a cloud of fragrance that smells fresh and green. It even smells yellow, don't ask me how, it just does.

We don't stay long after that, shops and things are not quite open. Baba stops at a service station to fuel up and buy water and drinks from the kiosk.

"What a change from the luxury of *Changamire*. But it also kind of feels like home." Chichi sighs as she shoves her bags under the bench that's become her bed and general living quarters. Baba gets in the driver's seat, Tana is up front with him. He calls through the partition, "All good back there? We're on the move!" And off we go.

CHAPTER TWENTY-TWO

ON my bench, trying to read, I doze off to the rumble of the truck. We're going to the last place on Baba's itinerary. Tana called Bingo yesterday when he saw a wildebeest from the deck of the houseboat. It wasn't really fair because he had a pair of binoculars that Kwame's father let them use, but that was his luck, I guess. The prize is fifty pounds. Baba said he would get it when we get back to England.

It's funny, I almost said, when we get back home, but it felt wrong somehow. I was born there, lived there, but for some reason I've been thinking of Zimbabwe as home for a long time and we don't even have a home here. I think it's because Mama and Baba also think of it as home. "I'm going home for two weeks," Mama would say. "I have to go home for a week or so," Baba would say, "there are some things I need to sort out." There were always things that needed sorting out here. Back in England things seem to

always be sorted. "No wahala," as Femi—a girl in my class—would say. No big deal.

I look out when the truck slows and stops. There's a police roadblock. I wonder what they're looking for. In the movies the roadblock is always to catch a fugitive or something, but here, every time we've stopped it's to check if we have a hundred things, including a fire extinguisher ee tee cee ee tee cee. Sometimes the cops just want to chitchat. They literally just chat for five or so minutes, asking where we're going, where the truck is from, is it hired, do we sleep in it, how fast it goes—all this while the queue behind us grows. Some people lose their patience and drive right around the police and their barriers and no one says anything. Baba says maybe they are plainclothes cops because otherwise they are taking a risk; sometimes up ahead will be a sharpshooter in the grass waiting for people who try to get away when they've been stopped. Baba is very patient; he has time to be in a good mood on the road, unless we've annoyed him.

Mama was also a very patient driver. She liked to put music on and sing along. She liked Afro beats and something called urban grooves from here. Sometimes she'd play some real golden oldies. She especially liked the songs that had our names in them, the names we used at school, not our Shona names. When she first took Chiwoniso to kindergarten, the teacher kept botching up her name. Mama said, "I don't know why she couldn't just read it the way it was spelled, because that's how you say it. She looked at it

and decided it was too foreign and she couldn't say it. It made me so angry. And for some reason, because this one teacher decided this, it seems they all went along with it—they just wouldn't try. So instead of fuming every time I had to talk to these teachers, I yielded. It wasn't a fight I wanted, so I registered all of you under your English names."

I'd asked her how come we had English names in the first place. Femi only had Nigerian names and most of the other kids only had one name. Mama said it was something they were used to from back home where children always had to be given a Christian name that was English, because of colonization years ago, and it stayed that way. It's normal, she said.

It didn't seem normal to me that someone who doesn't even know you would tell you how you have to name your children because they don't want to have to learn a word in your language. I wanted to know every language in the world, and so I decided that I did. I never once told myself that I didn't understand a language, I always listened, and even though I couldn't tell you exactly the words, I could understand what was being said. It wasn't hard for Caroline either. If you decide on something and you believe it—I mean, really believe it all the way down into your very first self where no one has told you anything yet—and you add it to all the things that have grown inside you, like it was always there, anything is possible. The trick after that is to doubt everything else for a while until it all gels—that's how you

get to the secret superhero place. Once you are there, there's no going back.

"Are we talking about Caroline?"

Meticais is wearing a shiny silver metal body plate that's tied front to back with leather straps on the sides. On their legs are nubuck chaps, around their neck it looks as if they stuck their head through a dense bush of light green leaves, and on top of this is a small yellow top hat with a black band.

"Are those really leaves, like, I mean . . . is it a real bush you got around your head?"

"What you should be asking is, is it a real head?"

"What do you mean?"

"If you think I am real then everything about me is real. If you think I'm not real then nothing about me is real. It's not up to me to tell you what's real and what's not. I'm just here for the story. Is it Caroline we're talking about?"

I mean, really? I give my head a little shake. For that matter, am I sleeping and dreaming that I'm awake and Meticais is sitting at the foot of my bench-bed? I can feel the truck moving and now I don't even know if I was awake or I dreamed the roadblock. I'm losing my mind.

"Am I dreaming?" I ask Meticais.

"You tell me," we say in unison, and they laugh their big big laugh that takes over the whole truck. This gives me an idea. I look across to the other bench and I don't see Chichi or the bench

even, instead I see the window-side of my room back in England. Outside, there is the glow of the streetlights.

"What if this has all been one long dream and we never came to Zimbabwe?"

"It's possible."

"No," I say, "we're not in England. I'm dreaming, but we're not in England."

"You confuse me," I say to Meticais, "because even when I'm awake you turn up and no one can see you but me, no one can hear you but me, and sometimes you even know what I've been saying all along even when you haven't been there."

"Do you know that I haven't always been there? Just because you don't see me doesn't mean I'm not there."

I've known this for a while now but I haven't really given it time.

"So nothing happens in my mind that you don't know about?"

"You tell me," we both say again. I laugh and shake my head. I'm beginning to understand.

"So why do you want me to tell you the stories if you already know them? And don't say, you tell me."

"Are you not the one who said, when it's not your story you can talk about it any way you want?"

"You tell me," I say.

"Ah! Touché." They reach up and tip their little hat at me. "It's not my job to tell you things, my dear, but I will do you a favor and

tell you this one thing. I'm not here because I'm dying to hear your stories, although they are very enlightening, if somewhat lengthy. I'm here because you're dying to tell them."

"Ha ha!" I say.

"Ha ha, indeed."

CHAPTER TWENTY-THREE

ONE day, we were driving back from The Program and Chichi phoned us. Well, she called Mama and Mama had it on the loudspeaker in the car.

"Mum, can we get pizza for dinner?"

"Mum said we could have Thai tonight," I replied to her.

"Yeah but I don't want Thai, do I though."

"You picked what we ate last time so this time it's my turn," I said. I didn't like it when Chichi did things like that. It made me really angry and I didn't want to fight with her. We had been getting along really well the past week and now she was being challenging.

"I'm not even talking to you. Mum, can you hear me?"

"Yes, Chichi."

"Well can't we get both then?"

"That's not how we do it, it's your sister's turn to choose."

"But Mum, if I order a pizza, it will get here before you do

with the Thai and I'm really hungry. I can't wait for you to get home. I just want to have something to eat and go to bed, it's been such a rubbish day."

"Have you done your homework?" This is what always happened, Mama was already giving in because otherwise Chichi would go on and on and she didn't have the patience for it. It wasn't fair.

"I did it at school already. Muuuuum!"

"She said no!" I yelled into the phone and hung the call up.

"Mati, why did you do that? That's not nice."

"Well it's not nice what she does, Mum. Why can't she stick to what we agree? It's not her turn to choose and she does this all the time because you let her."

"Oh, it's not a big deal."

"Yes it is! It is, Mama. It is, because it's not fair." I don't know why it wound me up so much. That's how Chichi always was so you'd think I'd have been used to it, but it was hard, so hard, because when she wasn't doing those things, she was really lovely and we'd be best friends, then she'd switch. She wasn't loyal and maybe that's what made me so mad.

But worse than Chichi was Mama. She didn't stand up to Chichi, it was like Chichi was the boss of all of us. It was easier to be angry with Mama than to have to fight Chichi when we got home, so I said, "Do you let her do what she wants because you feel guilty about almost getting rid of her?"

At first Mama looked confused, then her whole body stiffened

up and all the sound in the car disappeared into a far-away background. I know I shouldn't have said what I did, but I wasn't sorry. I didn't care that I wasn't supposed to know this, that I shouldn't have been eavesdropping, I just cared that Mama was not being fair. I expected her to tell me off, I was ready for it, but she looked at me with such disappointment and the words formed themselves in my mind, "I didn't expect this of you."

Instead she said, "Please don't ever tell your sister that." Then she stared straight ahead, tucked her lips away into her mouth, and didn't say another word to me.

When me and Caroline weren't watching movies, we listened to music. Caroline liked the vocals and the lyrics, I liked the backtrack. I liked to listen to it and hear each layer like I was seeing it and separating it, watching each part reveal itself—unmaking it, removing each layer until there's nothing—then I'd bring it all back again, drums, guitar, strings, brushes, the velocity, delays.

Some tracks swelled and made my heart feel like it was growing big and bigger, and then came back again on a string, like something suspended on a high line for a moment of indrawn breath, an exhale, then landing. That day in the car, I put my earphones on and played the song I always played when I felt angry—the guitar sounds like running, then jumping into a space full of things that twist and turn and spin you, until the feeling comes loose and paints the space, like fireworks. I'd open my eyes and let go of the

story of what happened. That's what I did in the car with Mama that day, or tried to do, but it didn't work.

When Baba came to talk to me before bed that night, I knew why it hadn't worked. Whenever Mama tucked her lips away into her mouth it meant that the words she wanted to say to you would come from Baba. I didn't like when this happened because that meant I would have to give answers to things I didn't want to talk about.

"Mati?" He knocked on the doorframe. "I'd like to talk to you."

I'd been sitting at my desk editing a video I'd made at the weekend. It was me and Tana walking in the park pretending we were in *The Blair Witch Project* when we found a bird that couldn't fly.

"Don't touch it," I say.

"It's hurt," Tana replies. I show his hands and the back of his head comes into view as he stoops to pick it up and then his hands again, this time with the small brown bird cupped inside them.

"It feels weird," he's saying, as Baba sat across from me on my bed and watched. The bird's tiny dark eyes are half closed, its feathers a thousand shades of brown and beige.

"It's dying," I say.

"I can feel fluttering, do you think that's the heart? Maybe it's not dying. Maybe we can save it."

"Put it back down," I say, "it's dying. Let it die in the leaves, your hands are not its home."

"Something will come and eat it if I put it down." Tana closes the bird in his hands until only the tiny head is visible.

In the end we agree to make a nest for it in the leaves underneath a tree. I pour a drop of water on a leaf and place it next to the bird. Tana is trying one last time.

"I can keep it warm until we get home. Baba will help mend it."

"It's only dying because we see it, because we say it's dying. It's being a bird and we know nothing about being a bird, let it be. Maybe it's going to a better place and it's happy."

"It's not nice to die," Tana says.

"How do you know? Have you ever died?"

The video cuts as Tana laughs, saying, "No, that's a silly question, Mati." He picks up a stick and walks on. "Have you ever died?" he scoffs.

I had been looking for a song to add to the end of the film for the credits when Baba knocked.

"You didn't want to try and save the bird?"

"I'm not a bird. I don't know that birds don't want to die. We don't have to decide everything all the time, some things don't need us."

"It's true, but we have the capacity to think and articulate our thoughts so it's natural that we believe we know more . . . better."

"We only know what we know."

"True, and we do the best we can with that and we never stop learning and discovering."

I turned to face him because I knew he was waiting for me to do that when he didn't say anything else.

"Mati, you hurt your mother's feelings today. She's very upset."

"I know."

"Did you apologize?" If I had, he wouldn't have been there. We both knew this, but we talk about things in a certain way.

"I was angry. She wasn't being fair."

"Do you think it's fair to talk to people about things that you heard in a conversation that wasn't for you to hear?"

That's why the song didn't work to help me let go of the story, because I can't get away from myself when I know I have not been fair.

"No," I said, "it's not fair."

"You're allowed to be angry when things aren't being done fairly, but you're not allowed to say things that have nothing to do with what's happening, especially things that not only are none of your business but also are things you couldn't ever understand because they didn't happen to you and you weren't there. Okay?"

"It's just a story," I mumbled.

"It's not your story to tell," he said. "Don't do it again." He got up and told me to start getting ready for bed. At the door he stopped and said, "Say sorry to your mother and then let it go."

I went to say sorry the next morning. Mama was in the kitchen.

As I was going down the stairs I heard Chichi and Tana in the living room.

"But Chichi, I got here first and the rule is that the one who gets to the TV first gets to watch what they want for an hour."

"Yeah, but Tana, I need to do my workout now cuz I got things to do later."

"You can use your tablet."

"No I can't. The big screen is better and there's more space in here. Come on, Tana. I'll give you two pounds to go spend in Aladdin's cave."

"I don't want two pounds, I want to watch my show."

"Tana! Come on, you can watch this show anytime. Record it."

"I don't want to." Tana had his days when if you looked behind him you would see that he was not happy about something. On those days you couldn't get him to do anything and it was best to leave it alone. I guess everyone gets into a mood sometimes, just because. He'd had a lot of activities at school that week so maybe he was tired and wanted to be left in peace.

"Muuuum!" Chichi called out. "Please talk to Tana. I need to do my workout before I go. He knows I always do it here, so why'd he start watching his show?"

"Fair is fair, Chichi. Mum, tell her." Tana defended himself.

I knew it would happen before it even happened and this made me angry all over again. Mama called out, "Tana, let your sister do her exercises. Come and help me decorate this cake I'm

making and later we'll go out for frozen yogurt. You can get all the toppings you like."

It wasn't fair what Mama did. She did this a lot because she didn't feel like arguing with Chichi and just wanted things to die down. Tana didn't know that before I got angry with Mama in the car we had talked about going out for yogurt that day so he hadn't won anything. Now I didn't even want to go, and I didn't want to say sorry anymore.

CHAPTER TWENTY-FOUR

WE'RE going to Baba's old village, where he grew up with his grandmother. This is one of the things he used to come home to sort out, when he came to Zimbabwe. Him and Babam'kuru Alois worked together to build it up for Gogo Mufanani so she could live in comfort before she died. We have never been there. This will be the first time. It's about three hours' drive out of Kariba near a place called Kazangarare. It's a fun name to say and we said it and said it until it started to sound like a crazy song. It was funny.

In the cab of the truck, we sing rounds and some silly camp song that Chichi leads and we follow, about a fly that flew right by and oomphed on everything in the grocer-man's shop. That grocer-man sounded like he was straight-up bonkers because he shot that fly right in the eye. But when I thought about it I realized that that grocer-man had to be someone who could see things in a way that no one else could, who believes a fly can be shot in the eye, and does just that—well, that's like a super villain. Every

superhero story has a super villain and up to now I hadn't really thought about that. Even a superhero can become a villain. There is nothing that cannot be changed in the secret superhero space because everything is possible.

"It usually happens when you lose yourself in your own sense of power."

Now that I'm not dozy and in and out of dreams, I remember Meticais's slight on the dam wall.

"What was all that on the wall this morning? Why did you act like you couldn't see me? I waved at you."

"That was your choice."

"I should have known not to bother."

"Listen, my dear, there are times when a person has to take time out for themselves. This was my moment and I wanted it just for me. I was the center of attention and I had that whole walk to myself. I was looking incredible, I had to take the moment." They take out their pipe.

"But no one can see you."

"So you think that because you are the only one in your family who sees me that you are the only one in all the wide spaces that surround you who I can see?"

"What do you mean?"

"I'm surprised at you, Matiponesa. Of all people, I would have thought you would know that what you see doesn't determine what I see. You know this about others, but not about yourself." This surprises me because I have never really thought about it like

that. Meticais takes out their pipe and lights up, watching me the whole time.

"Yes. You know it's true," they say.

"What do you think Caroline would have seen when she looked behind you? What story would she tell about you, do you think?"

Puff, puff. Puff, puff. I'm a second-hand ganky pipe smoker at this stage. I almost get a craving for it when it's not there.

"Why are you so obsessed with hearing about Caroline?"

"You tell me."

Ah man! I thought I'd gotten the better of the "you tell me" snag. Meticais smiles as if to say gotcha!

"Caroline's been gone so long," I say.

"Did she leave around the same time your mother died?"

My heart does the thing of rolling around like a loose stone on a cliffside and I'm breathless, my palms itch with pricklings of sweat.

"What did she say in the letter? Your mother?"

"What letter?"

"You said there was a letter she wrote, on the kitchen table, that might have explained everything."

"Oh yeah, there was."

"Did it explain things?"

"Goodness! I told that story so long ago now I can barely remember the details. It's all blurry now. So much has happened since that time."

"Is that right?" Puff. "Hmm."

I don't want to get into the discussion about "Hmm" again, so I'm quiet.

Then I say, "I'd have to start the story again, and probably then I'll remember all the details. It's not easy to just pick things out, they don't make sense otherwise."

"No no! Please don't do that."

I laugh then. "Gotcha!" I say.

"No you don't," they say. "You know it's time."

A story changes with each telling. Even a story about yourself. And even when you tell it differently to someone, there's always a part of you that knows the real truth. Sometimes we don't let that part speak. We keep it quiet and still in dark corners so only people who know to go behind things can look to see. It's not easy to go into your own behind spaces. You know you've hidden stuff in there but you can't remember where and it's the kind of stuff that can really give you flack and start to tell you that you're not who you think you are.

I always felt like Matiponesa, it's a name that felt like mine. Like I was always going to be Mati. But Mae? I don't know who that is. Mae is a ghost. When our cousins from Zimbabwe first came to visit us in England, they had a moment of disconnection when our English names came up because we've never had to know each other by them—they're outside names. They were like, "Ohhhhh! Mati, Chichi, and Tana are your crib names and those are your spy code-names so you can blend in. Of course! Like back home." We all had a laugh at that.

Yes! That was exactly it, but the funny thing is that while I used my name only to blend in and I was never Mae, Chichi was both her names. I don't want to talk about Caroline because I don't know what happened to her. When Chichi turned sixteen, Caroline started to disappear and after The Death, that was the end of her.

"She didn't die, right?"

"She disappeared."

"And why can't you tell that story?"

"Because that means I'm disappearing too."

CHAPTER TWENTY-FIVE

WE turn off the main road to head for Baba's village and if I ever thought the other stretch was the longest drive, now it is time for a new thought about that because the shaking and the tossing about we have to go through is more than a body can stand. I feel like a milkshake by the time Baba veers off the strips of worn-out tar and dust and plows through tall grass.

We're all craning our necks to see out the front because it looks like Baba is heading off into untamed bush with us, through a sea of the longest grass I have ever seen. It's coming all the way up to the windows and after about ten minutes the trees close in and close us up.

"Dad, I don't even see a road where you're going," Tana says. He's holding on to the bar across the dashboard and literally has his nose pressed to the windshield.

"Tana, sit back," Baba pushes him back with his arm across his chest. "If I brake suddenly, you will fly through the window."

There is a moment of absolute silence, but Tana sits back.

"We're going to stop for a little while before we get to the homestead. It's a place I used to come to as a boy. Not many people know about it."

We have to leave the truck a ways back. Baba packs a satchel with snacks and water and we carry a camping chair each—they are light and can be carried by a strap. Chichi fights the grass, the leaves, and insects all the way. Tana is wearing a hat with a net that can be pulled down across his face. I have no idea where he got it from, maybe from a jungle game set because it doesn't look very durable. He's so funny and sweet.

When he was born, I used to pretend he was my baby. When he was a toddler and would do something that annoyed me, I used to say, "I'm going to sell you to the rag and bone man"—something I heard in a film—but he would just laugh and show his few teeth and that would make me laugh because he had such a funny little face. I don't think I was ever angry with Tana. He likes shows about nature, and we'd watch them together, and sometimes when Mama was making her complicated recipes in the kitchen we would act like we were judges on *MasterChef* and taste everything and make remarks. We would laugh so much because of the words we found to describe things. We gave each other points for how many original words we could make up that sounded like they could be about food, like scrumpy and throgmollyfyingly obviliciously yum. I've never forgotten that one. It won a hundred points and was crowned the description of the season. Tana ran round the house

yelling, "Yessssss! Yesssss! Yessss!" Then came skidding onto his knees back into the kitchen like a football player, arms in the air, saying, "Champion!"

In the truck, on one of the afternoons, I watched him sleep, his face so soft and his whole body given in to wherever his mind had taken him. He twitched from time to time, like he was in some virtual reality game, but his breathing was soothing to me. I once told Chichi I liked watching Tana sleep because it made me feel like everything in the world was all right. Sometimes I used to let myself imagine where he went, what dreams he was having. I kept finding myself surrounded by dinosaurs. He laughed really loudly when I told him.

"Yes, you're always exploring in your dreams and you like the Jurassic period a lot. I don't really enjoy it."

"Mati, that's crazy," he said, then straight away, "what about space, do I ever go to space?"

"I don't know, you tell me," I said. "Don't you know your own dreams?"

"No," he said. And that was that for him. He didn't think about it anymore.

As we follow Baba into the trees, the vegetation becomes dense—more trees, more green—and it feels as if we are slowly closing ourselves in away from the world. I'm hoping there are no wild animals around when, as if he read my mind, Baba says, "Don't worry, it's completely safe here, you'll only see small game if you're lucky, no predators."

The quiet around us becomes really loud in my ears, only broken by the sounds we make as we clear our way through the overgrowth. We go from dry savannah into a place that feels tropical. We start to encounter rocks in our path, small ones at first and then they get bigger and bigger, and we climb a little, then all of a sudden, a clear and silent river. The water is flowing with gentle ripples in no hurry to go anywhere. The sun is shining through the trees and the trees are huddled around the banks as if they are hiding the river from everyone.

"Dad, are you sure we can be out here?" Chichi whispers.

"Yes, these are communal lands, but people tend to all live close to each other in certain places so here, is not so well known. We'll be perfectly fine."

"What are we going to do here, Dad?" Chichi asks, batting away little flying creatures from around her face.

"We're going to sit and breathe," said Baba, "and let our souls catch up with our bodies. It's been a long trip."

We climb down the other side of the rocks and there's a perfect beach big enough for all of us to find space to relax. The chairs sink into the sand, but it's okay. We follow Baba into the water and it's as if someone has whispered a magic word through our whole bodies that's made everything suddenly all right. After the dark coolness of the trees, the sun feels like magic on the tops of our heads. Birds coo and fish plop in the water. Insects buzz. Baba is right. I take a deep breath.

That night we camp like we did in Hwange, only there are no facilities. This is real camping, with a fire pit and everything. Baba cooks a fish he caught in the river, using a fish trap that he made of sticks and grass. "I used to do this all the time when I was younger." Tana is beside himself and he is eating the fish like a caveman who has just discovered meat.

"Like Bear Grylls, Dad," he says with a big grin.

"You mean, like everyone in the rural areas who has to catch wild game for their dinner," replies Chichi.

Baba laughs. I'm quiet. Being by the river displaced my soul. I'm still there, drifting. I know that it's the last peace we'll know. When we arrive at Baba's homestead, everything will change.

CHAPTER TWENTY-SIX

MAMA told me that she gave us English names from songs her father used to play at home. I was Maggie Mae, Tana was Dr. Robert F. Thomas—it's a song, I promise you, by an American singer called Dolly Parton. Kulu loved Dolly Parton, she said. And Chichi was Sweet Caroline. We found those songs online and we'd play them and joke about how those were our theme songs. These were the times when I loved Chichi the most, the times when she was my best friend. She was both her names. Chichi was my sister—fierce and a pain in the ass most times. Caroline was my friend—she really was sweet and she understood everything about how things were in my head. She found it funny when I called her sweet Caroline and even when she was Chichi, she knew I was never Mae. As for Tana, if he's Thomas, I haven't seen him yet. He's fully Tanatswa, so even at school when people call him Thomas, he hears Tana.

"What happened to Caroline?"

"I told you I don't know."

Today, Meticais is dressed in some pearlesque fabric that looks like a long night shirt. Their face is luminous like they have a filter again. In their ears are beaten silver disks and their dreads, hanging down to the floor, are studded with bedazzled cowry shells. I don't ask anymore about the looks, I just enjoy them. They are holding a beautiful crystal-studded shopping bag.

"It's for you," they say.

"For me?"

"What did I just say?"

"Okay." I reach out to take it but my hand goes right through it.

"You can't have it yet."

"Why?"

They give me a look that says, "I'm not even going to bother to say it," so with the biggest sigh ever, I say it myself: "You tell me!"

"You're starting to get the picture."

"Okay," I say, "okay."

That part of Chichi that was like me, it was a small part but the best part, for all of us. When she was sweet Caroline, we were all happy in the house and Mama never had to choose between us. When Chichi turned sixteen and started spending more time with Shaz, we saw less and less of Caroline and Chichi began to grow larger than life. Chichi was good for walking down the street with if there was someone you were scared of or if someone tried

to bully you at school, but at home she was too much of a "good" thing. Baba used to say this when the complaints got too much and he had to have a talk with her. "We love you Chiwoniso, you are a strong and feisty young woman. But that can be too much of a good thing. Have some mercy on us."

Shaz wasn't a bad person. She was different from the way we were. The way things were in their house—there was always a hurricane going on in there. I only went once with Chichi and I felt exhausted when we got home. It was like being on a plane when the turbulence doesn't end until you land—Shaz and her mum yelling at each other, slamming doors, and Shaz doing whatever she felt like. Chichi saw in Shaz what she could and couldn't be all at once—like a house cat with attitude, wanting to be a cheetah but knowing that's not how it was made. She tried anyway, and that's when we started to see less of Caroline. That's when Mama started to give in more and more.

One day I said, "Mum, why don't you tell Chichi she can't be friends with Shaz anymore? She's becoming someone we don't like."

"You don't like your sister?" She was at the sink wiping the big pot in which she'd made oxtail from the South African butchery in Luton; Auntie Monica had brought it with her when she visited at the weekend.

"I don't like how she is these days. It's like she doesn't care about anyone but herself and her friends."

"Do you think maybe it's more that you miss her?"

"I miss sweet Caroline, not Chichi."

Mama laughed. "Sweet Caroline," she said with a smile on her face, and started humming the song. "Makes me think of how my father used to play his records on Sundays and call us to come and dance. We knew all the words to his favorite songs. Did you know that Kulu was a headmaster? Not at the school I went to. Sometimes he was even headmaster at home. He could be so strict and then he could be so much fun, mostly at the weekends." She laughed. "We had a headmaster at home during the week and a father at the weekend. Sundays were always bittersweet for me."

"Yeah but Mum, that's not what we're talking about. We're talking about Chichi."

I didn't like when Mum—or anyone, really—changed subjects; otherwise the conversation never ended in my head.

"Do you really want to talk about that?"

"We have to talk about it."

"Do we?"

"Oh Mum!" I said. "Stop. I don't like it when you do that."

"Do what?" she said, but she knew what I meant. "Come," she opened her arm, "come and give me a hug, the complaints department is closed for the day."

Mama had many departments. The one I didn't love at all was the public relations department. We got this department when she was angry with one of us and didn't want everyone else to suffer for it, so she would be nice to you but you would know it was an empty jar. That's how Baba knew I hadn't said sorry to Mama

about my outburst in the car. He didn't say anything to me but that next morning at breakfast, he gave me a look that said, "You didn't do as I told you."

I wasn't angry anymore about Chichi being allowed to override the TV rule. I knew I wasn't allowed to be angry about a new thing before I said sorry about making someone else angry, so I had to let it go. It's so easy to let things go that it's frightening, and that's why we don't like to do it. We can't be sure of anything if we're not holding on to a feeling about someone else, especially anger, that's how we stay connected to our own sense of what is right. It feels good to be right. But I wasn't right, I had eavesdropped and then I had told a story that wasn't mine back to the person whose story it was when I didn't even know where it began or where it ended. That's not a story, it's a theft.

I'm starting to realize that my story of Mama does not make it her story. It's like a scrapbook, where you see pictures and letters and cards and you don't see that after the picture where people are blowing out the candles on the cake, the dog jumped onto it and no one got to eat the cake, and then the mum shouted at the dad for leaving the gate open that let the dog in, and the dad shouted back and the child started crying and nobody cleaned up the mess—but you go and tell a story that wow, they had a beautiful birthday cake, that child is so lucky, everyone must have had such a great time, what a great day they must have had. And that becomes the story you tell. And if they decide to, that's the story they'll tell themselves and each other—or they might decide to tell a different

one. It might be the day the mum decided she no longer loved the dad anymore because he never listened and that was the last straw and she'd had enough, and that's the story she would tell. The dad might say the mum was always finding things to yell about and that she never loved him because she didn't accept him the way he was and that she spent money on the party when they should have paid the rent. And the child? Shame for that child because that story would become mixed with other stories until the sky was the only sure thing. You can never know the whole story of everything, you take the pieces you're given and you fill in the rest.

CHAPTER TWENTY-SEVEN

BABA doesn't drive right up to the homestead. He stops on a rise and from a distance we watch the place. It's set up nice and neatly, with two small cottages facing each other across an open space that's a garden but also a place with two long benches and a table between. There are fruit trees all around and on the outer edge is a large, thatched hut. Around the whole homestead is a fence made of wooden posts and dried thorn branches. There are some cars parked outside and a tent behind one of the cottages facing the gate.

Tana crawls from his seat in the back to squeeze between Baba and Chichi in the front. They watch the people moving around the homestead for a while.

"I'm not ready," Chichi says.

"Me neither," Baba replies.

Chichi turns to look at Baba and tears are running down her face.

"It's been a tough year, Dad. I'm sorry I've been so difficult. I know you miss them, too."

Baba doesn't say anything, just turns to look out the window. He pulls Tana closer to him.

"I know Mati was your favorite. It's okay, cuz Mum was my favorite," Chichi says.

"What!" Baba laughs and Chichi joins in.

"I don't have favorites," Baba says. "Mati . . ." he sighs. "Well, Mati, she needed me more sometimes, that's all. She and Mum didn't always understand each other."

"It's because they were so alike," Chichi says, sniffing. "It was so strange. Mati would get so angry with me sometimes and I wouldn't even have done anything to her. It hadn't been great the last week. You know how Mati could just stop talking to everyone for days."

"She was reading a book in Arabic on her tab. She said the words made sense to her," Tana says.

"We used to do that, but with movies." Chichi smiles. "It was fun. We hadn't done it in a long time and that morning I don't know, I felt bad that I hadn't been spending time with her at all so I went into her room and got in bed with her before she'd fully woken up. I knew that if I waited, she'd wake up properly and remember she was cross with me. I showed her a funny reel on my iPad and then we edited subtitles onto a Japanese short film. We laughed and laughed even though it was about a very serious man who had a passion for flowers and a woman who didn't love him

back." Chichi is crying really hard now. "I gave her a hug. You know she didn't always like hugs, but she hugged me back and said, 'sweet Caroline,' and we laughed some more."

Baba pulls Chichi in so they're all squashed together. It looks uncomfortable but I guess it's okay for them because they stay like that for a while.

Tana says, "They were both my favorites. Mati used to play with me and we liked to watch shows together."

"I remember coming back home that day, Mama had left a note on the table. I don't even remember what it said."

"You read it," said Tana. "It said when these pies have cooled, please wrap them up and put them in the freezer, thanks, love you, Mum."

Chichi blows her nose and tries to wipe her eyes but it's no use.

"I don't think I ever did it. I don't even know what happened to them."

Tana takes her hand and says, "It's okay Chichi, I did it. I put them away."

Baba sighs. "I don't even remember if we ate them, there was so much food in the house after. People just kept bringing it for a while—your mum's friends." He rubs his face and I hear the scratch scratch of his whiskers. He hasn't shaved for a few days. That's what he does when he takes time to rest. He rests from everything about himself and only does what he has to do.

"So the note didn't explain anything, like you'd hoped it would?" Meticais is sitting with me in the bucket seats.

"Pies!" I say. "It should have said something more . . . something that would make sense of what was coming."

"But it didn't."

"Ssh!" I say.

It's good we took the time out to get here. To just be together as a family. Because when we arrive at the homestead it's really hectic. Our cousins are there and so are Babam'kuru Alois and Maiguru Anesu. Gogo and Kulu are there and even 'Nini Lisbet. Everyone is hugging and some are hugging and crying. We all go into the thatched rondavel and ask each other how we are. Chichi and Tana have to take their turn to ask all the grown-ups they are seeing for the first time. It's a whole thing. 'Nini Lisbet had a wrap ready for Chichi even though this time she wasn't wearing shorts and probably just as well because the men sit on a ledge around the rondavel and all the women sit on the floor. After all the greetings are done, the gathering breaks up. Baba goes off with Kulu and Babam'kuru and we go off with our cousins.

"You can't be here and not here at the same time," Meticais whispers.

"And yet here I am, am I not?"

"No need to get spicy," Meticais says and laughs. Then, "So! Here we both are," they say, "what next? Why did we make this journey?"

"Because the story wasn't done when everything changed. You can't just stop a story," I say.

"Oh, but that's exactly what happened. You think they know

what happened in the car that morning? What you might have said or not said to your mother before it all changed? You were in the car and you don't even know what happened, you only know the after."

"That's a big part of the story to have missing, don't you think?"

"Is that why you're here, then?" Meticais cocks their head and the cowry shells clatter against each other.

"Is that why *you're* here?" I reply.

"Am I here, though?"

At this I start to laugh uncontrollably. It's really ridiculous the things we say to each other. There's no winning.

"Does it matter?" I finally say.

"It could be the only thing that matters."

There is an outdoor kitchen that's open on all sides and has a roof and counters. All the cooking is done on a long grill where 'Nini Lisbet, Maiguru Anesu, and other women are busy with big pots. Baba, Chichi, and Tana are under a large muhacha tree watching a young man pull weeds from two mounds of flower-studded ground cover. There are plaques at the head of each mound. Me and Meticais sit on a large rock near one of the cottages and watch. A slight breeze passes from time to time and makes the shells clatter. We don't talk because suddenly it seems we're both of us not in the best of moods and I don't want to get wound up, but finally I say, "I saw it coming. I didn't want to say anything about it before because when it was about to happen, I knew . . . I knew there was nothing I could do to stop it and afterward, before

the sound came back, while it was still quiet, what I kept thinking was, who is going to know this part of the story?"

We sit on the boulder all afternoon and watch the goings-on. A priest arrives. Other people arrive. The priest lays out his things on the table that's been covered to make an altar. There are flowers everywhere. Chichi, Tana, and Baba change clothes and sit at the front in the tent. During mass they don't receive communion because we never learned to do that in England, even though all of Mama's family were church-lovers. I like the singing. The drums, the shakers, the high voices of the women and the deep chorus of the men: I like it and I wonder if I would have liked going to church.

"You're at church now," Meticais says.

"And I like it," I reply.

"That's all that matters," they say. We look at each other and smile.

When Baba stands up to speak, everything else falls away and there is only his voice. As if it is a warm current that surrounds me and pulls me in, I find myself standing at the edge of the tent, letting every word build me up from the very tips of my toes all the way up to the ends of my hair.

"Nine months ago, we lost my wife Mufaro and my daughter Matiponesa in a road traffic accident, on their way to school—a delivery truck failed to stop at an intersection and plowed right into them. Mufaro died on the spot. Matiponesa fought for her life for several hours but succumbed to her injuries without ever regaining

consciousness. I was on my way to meet them. I didn't know I would never see them alive again. Would I have done anything differently if I had known? I can't say. Perhaps I would have held on to them and not let them out of my sight, holding on, to let go another day. There is nothing we can do. As heartbreaking as it is, this is life. We never imagine that it will happen until it does. I'm used to being in charge, to saving a life when I'm called upon to do so . . ." For a minute, Baba cannot speak, he looks down. Then, wiping his eyes, he looks up and speaks again. "I have never felt so helpless."

Tana goes to Baba and wraps his arms around him. "You're a good doctor, Baba."

Chichi sits with her head down. 'Nini Lisbet puts an arm around her.

"Matiponesa was interesting, smart, funny, and so gifted. She had a way of looking at the world that opened our eyes to new thoughts and challenged everything we took for granted. She believed that we were all gifted beyond what we allowed ourselves to be and she was right. We will always hold on to this to keep encouraging ourselves and each other to be better every day. We miss her terribly." He stops to take a deep breath and waits a bit before continuing.

"Mufaro. The day I saw Mufaro is the first time I knew my heart. From that day on if I ever had a doubt about anything, it was never how I felt about my wife and the mother of my children. Even when I didn't understand what she was going through or

when she did things that angered me, even when we fought, there was never any doubt that I was with the only person for me. A part of me has gone forever and nine months on I know that we will survive it but life will never be the same again."

Chichi gets up to stand next to Baba and Tana. She takes a folded piece of paper from her pocket. She's changed out of her jeans and is wearing a floral summer dress with a cardigan. She clears her throat. She has a bunched-up tissue in one hand.

"I want to read something," she says. "My English teacher shared it with me when we went back to school and at first I was really annoyed with her cuz it felt like she was giving me extra work, you know, but I read it and when I think of my sister, Mati, I know that this is the exact right thing to say. It's from a sermon called 'The King of Terrors' by Henry Scott Holland.

Death is nothing at all. It does not count. I have only slipped away into the next room. Nothing has happened. Everything remains exactly as it was. I am I, and you are you, and the old life that we lived so fondly together is untouched, unchanged. Whatever we were to each other, that we are still. Call me by the old familiar name. Speak of me in the easy way which you always used. Put no difference into your tone. Wear no forced air of solemnity or sorrow. Laugh as we always laughed at the little jokes that we enjoyed together. Play, smile, think of me, pray for me. Let my name be ever the household word that it always was. Let it be spoken without an effort, without

the ghost of a shadow upon it. Life means all that it ever meant. It is the same as it ever was. There is absolute and unbroken continuity. What is this death but a negligible accident? Why should I be out of mind because I am out of sight? I am but waiting for you, for an interval, somewhere very near, just round the corner. All is well.

"All is not really well," Chichi says, sniffing and wiping her eyes, "but I know that wherever she is, all is well for Mati. Not even death will be able to limit her. She really is probably in the next room and is telling someone a long and detailed story as we speak."

At this, everyone laughs, and from behind me on the boulder Meticais's laugh is the loudest.

CHAPTER TWENTY-EIGHT

IN the car with Mama, with no other people there, the public relations department became the no-nonsense department. It was an open day at The Program, so Chichi and Tana went to school with Baba while we went ahead. Baba was coming along straight after. Mama turned up the radio to hear the news. They were talking about a police raid on a house in London that was a drug den. Mama acted like she was really interested in the story but I knew she wasn't. I should have just said it but I didn't want to shout above the news. It's annoying when you don't say sorry straight away and then it becomes a debt. I should not have gotten cross again the first time I went to say it. I could have let that go. It wasn't even about me, but about a stupid TV rule that Tana didn't even care about five seconds after licking cake icing from a spoon, in the kitchen with Mama. They were even laughing and singing a silly song, and Chichi was huffing and puffing at her exercises feeling her legs get toned, "as we speak."

"Look, Mati, look," she'd always say, "my muscle tone is improving as we speak."

I'd say it just before we got out of the car at The Program. It wasn't going to be the best time but at least I would have done it. I felt better now that I had made a decision, so I sat back and that's when I caught sight of the coin in the cubby between the seats. I remembered the day Armando was showing us coins from Mozambique. It was toward the end of lunch break in the quad. He had them in his pencil case for some reason.

"This one is quite old," he said. "I don't think it's in use anymore." It had a picture of a plant on it and said 10 Meticais. It was pretty and shiny, like it had never been used. The 10,000 Meticais had a rhino on it and was a dull silver. Caroline wasn't interested in the coins at all, she was busy taking a selfie of the three of us and trying to find the right angle. I was looking at the coins in Armando's hands, thinking how beautiful they were, well formed with clean neatly cut nails—perfect hands. I wanted him to hold out his hand so I could lay my cheek on it, close my eyes, and turn my face to the sun. Then he reached over, took my hand, dropped the 10 Meticais coin in, closed my fingers around it, and smiled. You will laugh, but right then, everything faded—my vision, my sense of time, of place, until there was only the sun making a halo around Armando's head and I heard angels singing.

I'm looking at the coin and thinking, that day was the last time

I saw Caroline because, later, while waiting for Mama to pick us up, Chichi said to me, "Why did Armando give you that coin?"

"I don't know, he was telling me that it was an old coin but special because it had stayed new all this time. He'd found it in an old box of things his dad had brought from Mozambique. They traveled a lot and he said his dad kept one box of things they always moved with no matter what."

"He said all that? While I was taking the photos?"

"And texting, and posting, and chatting."

"So if it's so special, why'd he give it to you, then?"

I shrugged.

"He must have seen the way you look at him."

"How do I look at him?" I said.

"Like you want him to hold you, and kiss you." She wrapped her arms around herself and started making kissy lips and sounds.

"Stop! You're being mean. You're the one who looks at him like that."

"I'm not denying he's cute and I'd date him, but anyway he likes Mariella."

"Here!" I took the coin from my pocket and gave it to her. "You're the one who's been talking to him, so you should have it." And I walked away cuz Mama was pulling up. The coin didn't feel so special anymore because of everything Chichi had said and anyway, fair is fair, Armando was her fish to begin with so I shouldn't have gotten any special present from him.

I saw Chichi put the coin in the cubby as she got in the car and immediately started telling Mama that she needed to get her hair rebraided in time for some party she'd been invited to and could we stop and buy the extensions on the way home. I left the coin there because of the Armando Accord.

"And that was the last you saw of Caroline."

"She was only Chichi after that."

I really don't know when Meticais changed, but now they are wearing, I don't know how I can say it, but quite literally, the night sky. Thousands of stars are imprinted on them on a fabric that looks like it's their skin because even their face is covered with it but still shows the lines and grooves. Around their face and on their head is an array of baby's breath, daisies, petunias, and something that smells like lemongrass. Trailing from the headdress all the way down to their feet and behind is a transparent gossamer curtain veined like the wings of a butterfly. We are back on the boulder. It's the best place to watch everything. Baba, Tana, and Chichi are sitting on a bench right below us, watching the homestead like we are.

"You were always only Matiponesa?"

"It's enough of a name, don't you think? To be everything all at once?"

"Do you think that's what the rest of your family would say?"

"Whatever they might say, I know one thing, I'm no less real now than I ever was. It's just that they can no longer look into me to find themselves, and they don't know what that means."

○   ○   ○

"You know, Dad, I was just thinking that it's just as well you and Mum knew what you wanted so early in your lives. You'd have had a lot less time together otherwise. I feel like I could have been a lot nicer and spent more time with Mati."

"You're never nice to anyone so I'm sure she didn't take it personally."

"Dad!"

Baba laughs and hugs Chichi to him.

"Remember how she called you sweet Caroline whenever you were getting along?"

"That was so silly, but fun. I don't know why she loved that song so much. It's so old. Sometimes I'd call her Maggie Mae and she'd say that Mae was an alias for a ghost that took her place in the English language. She was cute and funny like that, she saw things differently, was always creating new realities. She was so interesting."

"Her stories were always so long," Tana adds, "they almost never ended. She could tell a story for days and days."

Baba and Chichi laugh.

"You were sweet Caroline a lot more than you think," Baba says.

"Really?"

"Yes."

"You're always sweet Caroline to me," Tana says, and he means it. I don't know why he never sees Chichi any other way, even when

she upsets him. It doesn't take him long to hit the factory reset button. The moments he adores her are all that stay with him when all else is said and done.

"I haven't been her in such a long time, I think I'm a whole new person now. Not Chichi, not sweet Caroline, just Chi maybe, or Chiwoniso."

When the sunset comes, nobody has moved. Meticais hands me the bag.

"It's time to leave this place," they say.

"Why was I still here all this time?" I ask.

Meticais gives me a look.

"You tell me," I mutter under my breath.

The bag is light, as if there is nothing in there, but when I reach in I pull out a beautiful yellow jumpsuit of fabric so light it's almost liquid. Along with it is a cape of a million golden sparkles. It feels like it's moving as I touch it and I can't feel any threads holding it together. The shoes are incredible, glittery yellow and silver sneakers with big platform soles. They're soft and springy and I feel ten feet tall when I put them on. To be honest, I don't even know how it happens: I begin the act of putting them on, and then I'm fully clothed. My hair is adorned by dandelion heads that attach to every strand so that when a breeze picks up, a shower of white parachutes floats all around me.

"Wow! What is this made of?" I run my hand down the jumpsuit. The cape flutters around me.

"Dreams." Meticais rolls their eyes and I cut my eyes back at them.

"What do you want me to tell you? You're the one who brought me here and everything I come with comes from you. So if you don't know, then I don't know."

"You're a figment of my imagination?"

"Are you?"

"Not this again!" I huff, but there's no point because I know. I've always known, in the dark places where I keep my secret self, that I am more than all the stories I could ever tell about myself and there couldn't be enough lifetimes to tell it all because a story cannot really ever end until we know where it all begins.

EPILOGUE

IN the car with Mama, going to the open day at The Program, I picked up the coin in the cubby. I was looking at it trying to decide if I should keep it, and I was thinking that the coin was special to me not because of Armando, but because the time of being in love with Armando was the last, best time I'd had with sweet Caroline. She took the Armando Accord more seriously than me and by the time we sat with him that day at lunch, she had already started the Chichi and Shaz Shambolic Show—that's what I called it. I tossed the coin in the air and before I could catch it, there was a loud bang and the whole world turned over and over until there was silence. There was no up, no down, and all I could feel was my seat belt holding me in place. Something hissed and light came in from outside. I watched the dust settle. I saw Mama on her head, her eyes closed. I was so confused. In the corner of my eye I saw the coin lying on the roof of the car, between me and Mama, and then I saw them, sitting against the shattered glass of

the windshield, holding Mama's hand. Everything about them was shimmering—no colors, shimmering like sunlight on water. Even the face, weathered and so beautiful that my heart broke. They smiled at me and in my head I heard them say, "Penny for your thoughts."

"I was going to tell her, I'm sorry for what I said. I really was going to," I said.

They smiled at me and the last thing I thought, before my eyes closed, was that ten meticais was more than a penny.

ACKNOWLEDGMENTS

Thank you to Sarah Odedina at Accord Literary Agency for encouraging me to write this story—I thought I was done with fiction and would probably never have gone looking for Mati. Thank you Deborah Ahenkorah Osei-Agyekum, and thank you Simon Boughton for the thoughtful editing.

Thank you lovely Yeukayishe Musariri, my litmus test for all things YA. Thank you Mercy Msipa for the MS Office support. Every little bit of help matters.

ABOUT THE AUTHOR

BLESSING MUSARIRI is an award-winning author of short stories, children's stories, radio plays and screenplays, and contemporary adult fiction. Her work has also been published by the *Guardian*, *Granta*, and *Poetry International*. "Grief is not only about loved ones lost but about the life we who are left behind can no longer have," she says. "Of all my writing, Mati is my most luminous character. She brought Meticais along and these two together are my own farewell to a season of grief." Blessing lives in Harare, Zimbabwe.

ABOUT ACCORD BOOKS

Accord works with authors from across the African continent to provide support throughout the writing process and secure regional and international publishing and distribution for their works. We believe that stories are both life-affirming and life-enhancing, and we want to see a world where all children are delighted and enriched by incredible stories written by African authors.